Letters From a Rotten Log

Letters From a Rotten Log

Adventures of Cindi Camponotus, Carpenter Ant Reporter

ANTHONY PICARDI

outskirts
press

Dedication

To my uncle Joe, who taught me about insects.
To my mother, who took me to woods, beaches, fields and ponds.
To my wife, Shirley, whose brilliant editing will save me
untold embarrassment and who has the patience to live
with me and a carpenter ant.

Table of Contents

Introduction

This book is the result of a unique symbiotic relationship between a human (me) and a carpenter ant. The ant calls herself Cindi and self-identifies as a Camponotus, which is a genus of carpenter ants. I do not really know why she decided to communicate with me. Maybe she believes I can help her colony avoid the disasters that humans often visit upon other species. Or maybe she would like the respect that is due a family that now numbers 2.5 million ants for every single human on Earth.

What I do know is that her tribe has been listening to humans' rumblings and has felt and smelled the result during the whole of human evolution. Having learned our code, it was easy for her to take advantage of my computer, left on overnight, to send me the first message. This message was clear: "Do not use poisons. Leave us alone and we won't eat your house." I figured this was a credible threat coming from a carpenter ant since carpenter ants have a reputation for infesting wooden homes of the genus Homo. I wrote back and said that I would desist from chemical warfare if she would periodically report on what was happening under my nose around the farm. It is a quid pro quo deal that has lasted six years and has survived through several generations of erudite ants.

How does she do it? Luckily for Cindi, modern computer keyboards require only a light touch. Cindi can push down one key at a time by locking her legs under the keyboard around

a key. But she cannot do this while also holding down the shift. You will not find capital letters in her missives. Nor will you find question marks or exclamation points. I have chosen to preserve her style in the service of authenticity.

Can humans learn anything from Cindi's adventures? Both humans and ants are "eusocial" species, according to the greatest authority on ant sociobiology, the late E. O. Wilson. Put simply, eusocial species have evolved advanced social traits such as division of labor. They build homes which they defend as an organized group. Eusocial species care for members of their tribe, learn from each other, and communicate among themselves. In the case of the ant family, this communication is four-dimensional. Very few eusocial species have evolved since life began on Earth. Most are insects. After 168 million years, it seems almost inevitable that a member of the formicidae family —the taxonomic family that includes all ant species—would be the first to bridge the interspecific gap between ants and humans.

Cindi has a perspective about humans that is not always complimentary. Considering what humans have done to natural ecosystems, that is to be expected. Given enough time, she expects ants to outlive Homo sapiens. In spite of her attitude regarding humans, she often offers suggestions from her own perspective, should we find ourselves in the same predicament that she has experienced. Her suggestions often sound humorous. What do ants have to teach humans?

E. O. Wilson is quite emphatic on the issue of learning from ant civilizations. In the first paragraph of the first chapter of his latest book on ants, he states, "There is nothing I can even imagine in the lives of ants that we can or should emulate for our own moral betterment" (See *Tales from the Ant World*, Liveright Publishing Corp. 2020). I prefer a more nuanced attitude. While none of us like to be preached to by an ant, I would suggest that the application of a sense of humor to Cindi's adventures will help humans see the ridiculousness in some of our own behavior.

Having said that, I believe Cindi has an agenda. She is clear about it. She and her sisters aspire to rule Planet Earth after Homo sapiens are gone. They have been here for 168 million years and are playing a long game. There is some evidence that her carpenter ant sisters may be cooperating with some confederate ant species to nudge humans along the path to extinction faster than we will bring it about if left to our own devices. "An Epitaph for Humanity" published herein, is Cindi's indictment of Homo sapiens.

In addition, I sense a seething resentment among the ants beneath the mostly pacific and unseen interface between humans and our Formicidae fellow travelers. I found evidence for a conspiracy among different species of ants in a draft press release mistakenly left on my computer titled, "Ants Lead Global Conspiracy to Take Back the Earth," destined for the *New York Times* science section. I cannot imagine what would have happened if this had actually been printed in the Sunday *Times*. I have not so far found any other evidence of conspiracies. But who is looking and how would we, as humans, know? This collection of letters is the only high-level communication humans have ever had with the Formicidae family. Most of our interactions seem to be about the removal of crumbs from picnic tables. When you finish Cindi's missives, I think you will agree that we should keep our ears to the ground.

Finally, I think it proper to address the question of whether Cindi is my "friend." No. Not in the human sense of an empathetic friendship, or even a type of human-dog relationship. Rather, we are symbionts. I do not think that any insect, including a highly developed eusocial ant, could harbor an empathetic emotion pointed in the direction of Homo sapiens. There has been too much asymmetrical warfare between us and the ants. I believe her didactic moments derive from a desire to keep the quid pro quo going between us. This is how symbiotic relationships form and why they persist. They are transactional. What I also detect is a distinct attitude of "I told you so." I believe Cindi figures that when it is absolutely clear to all humans on earth that their days are numbered, she will laugh her gaster off all the way back to her colony and tell her sisters, "You heard it here first," like the inveterate reporter she is.

Tony Picardi
Williamsburg, Virginia
August 8, 2022

Suicide Mission

Editor's Note: "Suicide Mission" was first published online in *The Broadkill Review*, January 1, 2018.

september 2017

boss, are you trying to get me killed.

our deal was i will undertake certain surveillance and reporting assignments and you will refrain from chemical warfare on the estate. you asked me to get rid of the wasps. this is lethally dangerous. wasps eat ants for breakfast. the only way i could emerge as a whole carpenter ant, without being eaten by my relatives, was to assume a diplomatic guise and make contact in the cool of the evening during cocktails.

i set out for the white-faced paper wasp nest aka polistes comanchus.

sez i, 'evening, your white-faced regalness. may i have a word.'

'miniscule mite, i am a busy wasp with no time to banter with bugs,' she retorts, mandibles clicking.

sez i, 'your highness, i bear missives from homo sapiens management—owner of said porch roof wherein you repose and reproduce. he wishes that you pack up your hive and hightail it.'

'pernicious pest,' sez her white-assed queenness, 'we are a proud species with 100 million years of white-faced wasp supremacy in our blood. we build where we damn well please. don't need no stinking homos. avast, irksome bug.'

she flexes her big white abdomen, stinger pumping in and out.

begging your indulgence, excellency,' sez I, 'but management has classified you as an immigrant terrorist species hereabouts and declares that if you don't book a vespid vamoose he will unleash 'fire and fury and chemical death like the world has never seen.' homo management is a proud god who nukes what he does not love.'

'scram, you black-faced bastard before i separate your head from your thorax,' she screeches.

i left. next, i visited a dainty thread-waisted mud dauber, aka sceliphron caementarium, with yellow hose and stilettos, high-stepping in the mud of a hurricane puddle.

'what-ho, miss twiggy, what's with the high-rise hooves.'

'fashion, you little black trash,' she sez, with a sizzling sneer. 'our class of wasp is the proud owner of the shiny-ass-skinny-waist-yellow-decoration gene. i do not muddy myself with common slime.'

'tarted-up hexapod,' i complain, 'management god wants you to cease and desist with the spider-stuffed mud-huts in his boats and weather station.'

'little incubus, you may tell management god that the beautiful submit to no higher power. we are pretty-proud. scram,' she yells, skinny legs wobbling as stilettos sink into the mud.

not dead yet, i scampered off to the watermelon-sized abode of the immigrant european hornets aka vespa crabro.

'hellooooo in there, anyone home. i would speak with your queen.'

'who trespasses on this sacred monument,' croaked a gravelly-voiced, shredded-winged, and worn-out specimen of vespa crabro as she creaked around the side of the honorific hornet house.

'begging your pardon, your dignity. i come in peace to see what it would take to get your tribe to decamp,' sez i.

'we are dead, you stupid ant,' huffed her haughtiness. 'you are standing on the mausoleum of the bravest. the monument to our fallen heroes at our proudest hour [cough]. the day we raided yonder beehive, killed everyone, and stole the honey [cough]. it was a day of glorious, gory genocide. it was a day when the weaker, meeker immigrant bees were extirpated [cough]. their larvae felt the bite of our merciless mandibles [cough]. their decapitated bodies lay in heaps in front of their ugly painted wooden slum. the superior species conquered all [cough cough].'

not a little annoyed by the fathomless arrogance of this speech, i responded, 'yet i observe, your haughtiness, that there is no one left drinking cocktails on the porch of said sacred sarcophagus.'

'ant-imp,' she retorted, becoming breathless, coughing, abdomen pulsing, 'we rose to such exalted heights of greatness that the jealous gods took their revenge and gaaaaaaaaaaas-ssed us [wracking cough].'

boss, i can see you now, standing there in your bee bonnet unleashing an angry stream of 'raid' into the dark hole of this hornets' nest. they paid for their savagery, and this old termagant will tumble to the ground and rot in her hubris. so i let it slide that she, too, was an immigrant—her clan having debarked in new york no sooner than 1850.

i have endured insults, threats, and savage mockery even as i comported myself as a civilized emissary. you have an attitude problem in the neighborhood. these wasps trespass upon your patience and physical infrastructure with a genetic conceit. pride is the tragic flaw of the wasp family.

but be merciful. i advise against all-out war, boss. don't let your superior armaments lead you down the slippery slope to neighborhood bullyness. it will corrode your self-esteem and i will have to quit. as my great-great-great-great-ant once said, 'deplorable wasps ye shall always have among ye.'

i suggest a solution that will benefit both of us. act like a sensitive homo management god and judiciously apply some tactical 'raid' to the offending vespinae domiciles. in exchange, we will not eat your house.

Anthony Picardi

factually reported and respectfully submitted as per agreement by cindi camponotus, official holly point farm investigative reporter

Stink Bug Supremes

october 11, 2017

boss, the stink bugs are irrupting.

investigating the source of the rasping and chanting under a poison ivy vine, i made the acquaintance of 'stinky and his cabinet' wailing away, accompanied by 'the katydid acrimonies.' i recorded some of the words in case you want to know who is raising the stink and why. katydids only sing in one note, as you can see from the lyrics. i quote,

she's a bum
zero sum.
look down
let 'em drown.
no more aid
we're afraid.
life is crap
you're a sap
in a trap.
aliens
closing in.
build a wall
very tall.

"build a wall! aliens closing in!"

grab more
for yourself
us first
eat the poor.
send a tweet
indiscreet.
sentences
incomplete.
set us free
you and me.
deport
build a fort.
play some golf
trump resort.
label them
libel them
muffle them.
game them
frame them
blame them.
hate them
shackle them
prison them.
cry out
mean shout
mega pout.
grab them
push them
bully them
punch them.
enemies
conspiracies.
blood spilt

no guilt.
tribal day
shame away.
courtesy
not today.
protocol
not our way.
tv show
opticals
steal the day.
facebook
have a look.
you choose
fake news.
have some lies
with your fries.
empower us
pardon us.
wrath storm
nonconform
new norm.
leader say
it's okay.
rally us
tally us
lie to us
anger us
answer us
swear to us
avenge us
promise us
savior us
bless us.

it went on and on. i investigated. it first appeared that these stinkers were just putting out a rap-track to extract lucre from the rest of their odious clan. but no. there is much more.

this is being piped into the deep dark web of underground hate chants. i traced it on your pc and it came out at a homo sapiens rally.

boss, i don't want to sound superior, but we have seen this before. it happens every time one of your dictators goes mental and sets one group of homos against another. chaos and killing result. you are the only species that kills your own kind - sometimes in spectacular numbers. and now we know why. you are the unwitting victims of a stink bug conspiracy. it sows intra-specific wrath which will compel you to commit yet another genocide. think about your epitaph, 'here lies homo sapiens, superficially intelligent, succumbed to weaponized wrath.' what are you going to do about that.

factually reported by cindi camponotus, official holly point farm investigative reporter

3

Light Shown on the Dark Web

Editor's Note: Alarmed by Cindi's report on the irruption of stink bugs, I wrote this press release for publication in the *New York Times* in May 2018. It was never published because neither Dr. Herodias nor the author of the ominous report could be found for verification.

May 2018

Global Network Disseminates Divisive Discourse
Rogue Stink Bugs Compose Lyrics for Trump Rallies

By Dr. Tony Picardi

Belle Haven, Virginia. – In an astounding feat of investigative reporting, a recluse lepidopterist on the Eastern Shore of Virginia has found the source of hate speech in America. Citing an anonymous source, Dr. Cyaneous Herodias, wildlife refuge manager at Holly Point Farm, has determined that contents of the speeches given by Donald Trump, President of the Electoral College of the United States, can be sourced to a vast underground network, until now known only to software nerds. They call it the deep dark Web. Dr. Herodias's

12

vast background in software architectures and complex dynamic feedback systems has enabled him to penetrate the biogeochemical pathways that form the basis of this "dark Web."

"We are dealing with a superorganism consisting of adaptive autonomous agents that communicate via coded messages superimposed upon the monotonic raspings of katydids," said Dr. Herodias. When asked to explain how these messages could travel, Dr. Herodias elaborated, "This interspecific communication system is much like the human method of sending Internet content packets over your phone lines, otherwise known as DSL. The rasping song of a katydid travels through the air and resonates within the surrounding vegetation and is picked up by other katydids through audio receptors in their legs. This packet relay method sends messages wherever katydids are heard, even into outer space."

Stink of Collusion

In the past several years, divisive rhetoric has been used by the Trump campaign and now the White House to rally his following of white supremacists and willfully ignorant nationalists to support his benighted narcissism. But from where do these deplorable declarations originate? Dr. Herodias has evidence gleaned from a report written by the refuge staff. The existence of this report has been verified, but Herodias has withheld the author(s) name(s) to "prevent them from being stepped on."

In an ironic and poetic twist of literary serendipity, it appears that the odious chants at Trump rallies have been authored by a species of insect called the stink bug. Through his sources,

Dr. Herodias traced the latest eruption of hate speech to a species known to science as Euschistus variolarius, aka the one-spotted stinker. Said Dr. Herodias, "Stink bugs kill their prey by sucking them dry. The variolarius is a particularly noxious violator of violets and sucker of soybeans. It is a pest."

Asked to comment on how the stinking lyrics become superimposed upon the monotonic strains of the katydid, Dr. Herodias explained that his sources caught a recording session "in vivo" on his refuge. "It is a curious collusion of creepy creatures. We know that the stink bug songster group is called 'Stinky and His Cabinet.' They collude closely with a chorus of katydids that call themselves 'The Katydid Acrimonies.'" The superimposition of medium and message is apparently a potent technological advance, allowing much more complex messages to be broadcast relative to the tweet, heretofore the medium of choice for birdbrains.

Deliverance?

Hoping to fathom the depths of depravity to which stink bugs may sink, the good Dr. Herodias arrested a number of them for interrogation. Under the persuasive influence of ethyl acetate, stink bug number sixty-seven spilled the beans.

Quoting Dr. Herodias, "It appears that many species of

Stink bug sixty-seven

stink bugs are colluding to embed chaos, fear and hysteria in the dark abyss of Homo sapiens' id." Asked for the reason, Dr. Herodias demurred, "I cannot speculate as to the reason why several orders of insects should rebel against humans, for fear of losing my reputation for scientific objectivity. But what I am hearing could be a threat to our national security." Reading from the testimony of witnesses to the recording session, it appears that stink bugs are attempting to nudge Homo sapiens into another great genocide even greater than the last one. These sources claim to have observed humans from our beginnings.

Dr. Herodias quoted from the report, "Here lies Homo sapiens, superficially intelligent, succumbed to weaponized wrath."

I Bought a Submarine

Editor's Note: "I Bought a Submarine" was first published in *The Broadkill Review*, September 1, 2018.

summer 2018

boss, you are not answering your email, so i decided to help you out where my invertebrate reporting and the unique perspective of a carpenter ant will be illuminating. don't worry, on the internet, nobody knows you are an ant. even though i can't operate the shift key, folks will just think you are lazy, which, for you, is logical.

you got a note from your financial advisor about your 6-months portfolio tune-up. i took the meeting. he opened with the standard wall street party line about diversification, consumer non-discretionary staples and gold in a time of uncertainty. i observed that my dark underground network is calling for a recession and a war within the next two years and that you needed to move beyond toilet paper and doubloons.

so now you own a very small share in an advanced nuclear submarine—the kind that can go anywhere undetected and that will appreciate as the war heats up. it is the 'wave' of the future. it is where the smart money is hunkering down.

it is an opportunistic monetization of the latest budget rec-onciliation bill which included privatization of individual mili-tary assets to reduce costs, eliminate needless regulation, and create jobs. You are still invested in toilet paper, but it seemed reasonable to hedge in the direction of 'the big one.'

you should feel better now knowing that, as an angel inves-tor, the sub—i cannot tell you its name online—will make a drive-by in occohannock creek next week on its way back from the coast of north korea to annapolis and then new lon-don. also, you get priority defense in case a chinese container ship, which btw we can see from the dock, tries to 'sneak up the creek' so to speak, and loses overboard a container of fake rubber dolls made to look like the grabber-in-chief with ersatz orange hair. that would contaminate the creek and mess up the fishing, boss.

so yes, i have extended our defensive perimeter way beyond the range of your puny personal firearms arsenal, which, in my opinion, is irrelevant when the missiles start to fly.

your submarine security will pay greater dividends on the run up to the next war, validating the mathematical expression

ammo plus gold plus nukes = security.

amazing how a little defense makes you feel secure. in our underground network, we are no longer scared. you should be as happy as a harp seal at a sushi bar.

i leave you with this gratuitous advice on the morning of the evening of your civilization—

Our sub will sail up the creek next week

'those who anticipate the fire and fury carry extra toilet paper in their subs.'

with great expectations for your financial future, i am, cindi camponotus, financial advisor and official holly point farm investigative reporter

Spies in the Woods

may 2018

the fbi—the feral bird investigators—found them in the woods travelling south. our red, white, and blue team of jays, cardinals, and bluebirds had lined them up for execution by mastication. i interrogated to see if they were alien invasives or spies. if spies, this could be evidence of a larger infestation. and you would need more than pesticides to cope with them.

i could tell by their ushanka hats they were russians. i assumed they were spies on a mission. i spoke to them from an overhanging branch, invoking the spine-chilling fear, if not the actual accent, of an fsb officer.

'little tarakans, you are running through the woods like scared babushkas. why do you desert your post, you cowardly capitalist roaches.'

the spies staggered around, looking up into the trees by rising up on four legs—since cockroaches' necks don't bend upward—searching for their leader. i assumed they never actually met vladimir vladimirovich, so played them fast and loose.

Their hats indicated they were Russian spies

'i send you to get kompromat on orange leader. you get lost in woods.'

'not lost, volodya, going into exile at merry lago,' said felix, apparently the head apparatchik. i decided to make an example of felix.

'lying to fbi is getting you eaten, comrades.' a blue jay pecked up and swallowed felix head first. the rest sang like crickets on a hot humid night. the tale was bizarre.

'is like you predict, volodya. operation moose and fox is glorious caper for sending propaganda to world. we report to general flynflam. general arrested for being spy. are we all going to spy gulag. orange leader saves us with excellent propaganda. we work between sheets doing cheeseburger tweeting. foxes beam to moose. moose calls fat cats. fat cats confuse moose. roaches whisper to moose from orange hair nest. moose tweets. fox plays tweets on tv. it is glorious propaganda. is biggest most excellent secret-leaking operation to world, volodya.'

'then comes trouble with queen. queen declares war on roaches. queen locks us in moose bedroom. she is not wanting russian roaches or leaking moose in her bedroom. queen says she had too many leaking roaches in slovenia. 'het to moose in bed,' she says.'

'moose denies us. moose rips off sheets each morning looking for golden rain leaks on sheets. sends us flying with fries, catsup, and cokes. next grigori rasputin-boltonov turns everyone radioactive with nasty leaking book. boltonov sent to gulag by general. we are afraid we mutate into hillaries and get sent to prison. is chaos. is war coming. we chew and flush moose and fox plan down golden toilet. need to leave before we get radioactive and burned to crispy spy fries. orange leader promises general flynflam pardon...but not us. we want to be oligarchs, not gulag prisoners. send money, volodya.'

determined to burnish my bona fides in counterintelligence, i sowed disinformation among these spies. 'comrades, go south to merry lago. look for american dream. email message to oligarchs —'send rubles for moose and fox campaign. ship rubles in washing machines to merry lago.' tweet moose, 'washing machines needed for washing kompromat from sheets.'

i advised them to hitch a ride on a chicken truck when they got to the bay bridge tunnel. i told them, 'tell the chickens not to eat you because they are going to chicken heaven and there will be a big celebration at chick-fil-a.'

humming the 'marche slav,' the little band of spies marched into the shadows of our pine-oak forest surrounded by a hungry fbi. whether they will make it out of the woods, survive the panicked chickens on 'tyson's tender transport' and live to become oligarchs is a question answerable only by the fbi and mother nature.

if they get to merry lago, vladimirovich will be pleased by my creative money laundering scheme. i sent an email to comrade mueller telling him to look for washing machines coming from cyprus filled with rubles. don't worry, boss, i routed the email through north korea.

Anthony Picardi

as i write this, i imagine your moose is going mad stripping his bed, looking for roaches after talking to foxes all night. i chuckle. homo sapiens americanus is infested. we don't have this chaos in ant colonies under the leadership of an ant queen. she uses pheromones that tell the truth, not like propaganda. we extirpated one band of spies for you. boss, you are infested. there will be more if your tribe of big thinkers doesn't do something soon.

factually reported and respectfully submitted as per agreement by cindi camponotus, official holly point farm investigative reporter and head of the fbi

An Epidemic of Fake Sex

june 2018

why did you end up with a national drone instead of a queen mother.

i have focused my investigative powers on the last mating dance between your orange drone and your white queen—called a 'presidential campaign debate.' it was an abysmal display of ineffectual and unconvincing sexual conflict from which there has been no intelligent issue.

boss, you have an epidemic of fake sex. here is my report.

first question. why would you grab a female's sex organ without consummating the act. it makes no sense. your drone needs a lesson from the fruit flies. fruit flies are called fruit flies for a reason. a lot of them are fruits. in fruitflyland older males teach virgin males the art of copulating. graduates have a measurably greater success rate with the fairer flies, as measured by your own national institutes of health. in the dead of night, maybe your drone needs to watch a little fruit tv.

or maybe his pusillanimous grabbing is ignorance. for this i suggest a lesson in dragonfly courtship. here is a case, boss, where foreplay results in sex that is guaranteed to count for the home team. your male dragonfly begins by clearing the decks—scraping out the semen sacks of all previous suitors. he loads his precious bodily fluids into his paramour, and the fun begins. your lusty odonata grasps his queen by the neck and splashes her on the surface of the pond so he can be sure her released eggs are only paired with his swimmers. now imagine if your drone, having mastered the art of fruit fly foreplay, had employed this salem witch-dunking maneuver—took his queen by the neck and dunked her in the potomac while simultaneously inseminating her. rough sex, yes, but the fans would have loved it.

suppose your drone is more romantically inclined. for that i suggest a lesson from the lascivious bowerbird. some of them even have orange topknots. the bowerbird dances on a branch, spins, flutters, spreads his topknot, splays his tail, puffs his chest, jumps, somersaults, and exercises himself to exhaustion. there is no groping. his intended mate watches, aloof, judging his act for evidence of superior genetic traits, and makes her choice.

instead of his shambolic lurking and creeping in back of his queen so she couldn't even see him, imagine the scene on the global courting stage if your orange-plumed national drone danced and cartwheeled on a limb while singing love songs to the aloof, cold-hearted queen in a white pants suit. that's the kind of display you could believe in.

but we both know this is impossible, boss. a drone is a drone. the last time one of our drones proffered a lustful antenna at

Cindi suggests dragonfly courtship for humans

me, i bit off his head. it resides now along with his corpulent corpse on our community trash heap—the fate of so many fake lovers everywhere. males that are simply a lorica for the y chromosome usually meet an inglorious fate. your mantid male gets devoured after intercourse. your male black widow spider gets chewed up and sucked dry. your saturniid moth emerges beautiful, has sex and dies, shriveled from starvation.

given the well-known failure of your drones in the love department, is it any wonder that an increasing number of your females are resorting to sperm banks where proof of product exists. why risk questionable genetics. why not get back to basics—what is sex for in the first place if not for producing the fittest folks. is this the beginning of intelligent design lead by your fertile queens.

without the creativity to compose a sonnet or the competence to complete copulation on the global dance stage, your drone is doomed to genetic death. this is why we ants have wisely elected queens to rule the hive—manufactured them actually. when our queen puts out a chemical message, it permeates, we get it, and we march. we are united. periodically we are invaded by red army ants who spray mimic alarm pheromones around our hive to disorient us while they pick off our soldiers. as our defenders run amok, the reds carry off our larvae to enslave them. it's chemical warfare. but our queen puts out the truth pheromone and rallies the troops. our superorganism survives. our species has survived over 168 million years. there are now over a 2.5 million ants for every homo sapiens alive. do the math, boss.

i don't know another social species that has a drone in charge. is homo sapiens doomed. probably. a species can't obsess on fake sex, ignore the science of competitive courtship and expect to survive for long. sad for homo sapiens. happy for the rest of us.

factually reported and respectfully submitted as per agreement by cindi camponotus, official holly point farm investigative reporter

Treason

Editor's Note: "Treason" was first published in *The Dead Mule School of Southern Literature,* February 2019.

october 2018

boss, i always thought homo sapiens was the species with the greatest capacity for destructive self-delusion and corruption. in our symbiotic relationship, i laboriously push your computer keys one at a time all night to report local farm events. i have reported stink bugs in the deep state. i have intercepted spies in your woods. but yesterday the corrosive clouds of conspiracy thundered over my own carpenter ant colony. i was summoned to the queen's chamber. i trembled in my exoskeleton. i was commanded to investigate and prosecute the case of the missing children.

the colony is roiled by rumors of missing children, kidnapping, aliens infesting tunnels, babies dragged off and devoured. hysteria reigns. mischief is loosed. it could be six-footed. the queen doused me with royal pheromone scent. this gave me access to all colony chambers and a passport to the elites. here is the transcript of my investigation.

i started in the nursery. forensics showed that the piles of shredded exoskeletons in the corridors were ant larvae. dna showed they were camponotus—our clan of carpenter ants. you can't get into the nursery without smelling like a nurse ant. i interrogated the head nurse.

cindi—are you sure no aliens have been admitted to the nursery.

nurse—absolutely. no one gets in without passing the sniff test.

cindi—how about antennae bumps. is that required all the time.

nurse—not all the time. larvae don't have antennae.

cindi—so it is possible that an alien could have entered the nursery, smelling like a camponotus but feeling like a larva.

nurse—that's right. a few days ago, we had a really big visitor, but it disappeared.

i found a nursery guard and questioned her in the dismemberment interrogation chamber.

cindi—were you on duty this past week.

guard—yes ma'am.

cindi—did you smell a large visitor enter the nursery with no antennae.

guard—yeah. large bloke came through a week ago. nothin' unusual. smelled okay.

cindi—how large.

guard—two and a half ants.

cindi—how many legs.

guard—dunno. didn't count 'em.

cindi—let me help you remember.

i motioned to my sergeant to bite off one of her tibia for the purpose of memory enhancement.

guard—ouch. okay, there were six up front and a bunch of bumps in the rear.

cindi—when this visitor left, where did it go.

guard—after a few days, it climbed up the bush over there.

i followed a strangely sweet scent trail out of the colony, up a bush, and out onto a twig. there was a chrysalis, mute, immobile and disguised as a dead leaf. the suspect hung out in plain sight, mocking its victims below. i posted a guard armed with a royal subpoena and with instructions to arrest the suspect after it emerged and before its wings dried. it was a flight risk. your sherlock holmes used to say, 'when all the possibilities have been exhausted, whatever is left, however improbable, has got to be the truth.' the truth was we had been attacked by a feniseca tarquinius, the harvester butterfly, notorious consumer of aphids. this beast is the only carnivorous butterfly in north america. of all the colonies in all the states in this country, this rogue had to wander into ours.

but something wasn't right. the larval tarquinius lives among and devours aphids for lunch. no science says it sucks on ant larvae. how did this terrorist tarquinius acquire the secret smell that admitted it to our colony. was this the act of a lone mutant freak or a conspiracy between colony sisters and a foreign adversary. i suspected i was dealing with collusion to defraud the defenses of the hive with lethal consequences. a carnivorous lepidoptera had entered the nursery with the premeditated intent to consume larvae. in this caper, some of my sisters were at least unwitting co-conspirators.

i staked out the shipping and receiving tunnels where foragers returning from all directions were unloading pieces of rotten fruit, crumbs, assorted parts of dead insects, and a protesting, legless grasshopper, which was carried by three soldiers. sometimes a forager would return looking quite happy but with empty mandibles. a few arrived together in a conspicuous cacophony of comradery. i intercepted them.

cindi—avast nestmates. why do you return home with nothing to share with your sisters.

1st forager—arrrgh not empty. we are loaded to the gunwales with sweet nectar from yon floozie in the bushes.

2nd forager—you want to sample 'er wares, see scarface.

3rd forager—we been protecting her from ambush bugs.

i backtracked on the trail of the sugar-high revelers to a small beech tree. i climbed up and out to new growth where a dozen ants were standing guard over a small herd of aphids. in the midst of the aphids was a whiteish caterpillar with orange

The treasonous aphid herders

fuzz and green spots. the ants took turns licking droplets secreted from the rear of the caterpillar. another ant caressed the caterpillar with her antennae and rubbed her abdomen on the corpulent slug, coaxing more secretions from its nether region. all the while, the caterpillar masticated aphids—their bodily fluids dripping from its face in a disgusting display of gluttony. horrified, i realized this was the creation of a spy. it was secreting honeydew from its anus to compromise our guards. whatever the caterpillar wanted, our guards willingly supplied. a scar-faced ant approached.

scarface—arrrgh sister, you want some butt, pay up and get in line.

cindi—pay up, i asked.

scarface—one aphid per minute...in advance.

cindi—so...i thought you folks were supposed to be herding aphids. is this caterpillar stroking legal.

scarface—don't give me your legal mouthwash, sister. this is the quid pro quo game. you stroke the worm, you get the good stuff. when the worm gets fat enough and smells like us, we sneak it back into the hive and charge admission.

cindi—whoa. you escort this fat dude back inside the colony.

scarface—what's the harm of a little off-the-books business. and don't think you're gonna be a hero, sister. once you suck some butt, you are one of us. if you sing to the queen, we'll come after you—you'll be toast, hon.

i appreciated the frankness of scarface's explanation of how i would be compromised and thenceforth inhibited from spilling the beans on their off-the-books business, protection scheme and caterpillar stroking. i was never inclined to lap 'whatever' from the anus of a caterpillar anyway, so i wasn't compromised. but i couldn't arrest this criminal mob all by myself. i retreated and used my royal writ to send the 'cops'—the camponotus operations and protection service—to round up the gang of conspirators. the cops assembled the suspects in the dismemberment interrogation chamber.

cindi—did you knowingly aid and abet the admission of aliens into the colony.

scarface—it ain't illegal if a creature walks in on its own six pins.

cindi—i didn't ask for your bogus, self-serving legal ignorance. each time you lie to the prosecutor, you will lose a leg. answer the question.

i nodded to the sergeant-at-arms, who bit off scarface's right rear tibia at the thorax.

scarface—ouch. we just laid some stink on them so we could bring them back and set up a sucking stand.

cindi—did you accept payment or any other emoluments in exchange for your help in entering the colony.

scarface—oh no.

i nodded to the sergeant, who bit off scarface's left rear tibia.

scarface—ouch, she exclaimed. well, the worm gave us

honeydew if we stroked it.

cindi—how many were in on this scheme.

scarface—i dunno. just me and the girls.

i nodded again. scarface lost her middle right tibia.

scarface—ouch. i remember now, it was all of the guards on the aphid rotation...about 300.

at this point the queen and her escort marched in shouting, 'treason, treason, off with their heads, off with their heads.'

the wheels of justice screeched to a halt, after three legs, on account of the queen's impatience and desire to get back to egg laying.

'hear me,' she commanded, 'i will not have treason. i will not have a witch hunt distracting the orderly operations of my colony. round up the entire aphid patrol and purge them,' she shouted.

i was called aside. 'dump their carcasses in the trash heap,' hissed the exasperated queen. the queen felt her legitimacy would be threatened if she was seen to treat treason tenderly. she would cleanse the gene pool forthwith. i ordered the colony guards to round up the honey-sucking aphid patrol and extirpate the lot of them, along with their lawyers, without further trials. it was an efficient operation. in the presence of the queen, i demurred as to whether some clueless sister would ingest the traitors' dead carcass pieces from the trash heap and thus be infected with treacherous, treasonous tendencies. when the 'night of the great purgation' was over, the queen discharged me from my duties as special investigator with a commendation for meritorious service.

boss, i am very worried. how did we miss this. who would have known that a cute little butterfly could have such nasty adolescent offspring. even worse, what possesses a normal middle-class ant, raised in the lap of formicidae eusocialism, to compromise her sacred democratic values and commit treason.

i am afraid the queen's swift justice accomplished little beyond the optics of rescuing some baby ants. we are all sisters, descended from the queen herself. we all share the same gene pool. we all have in our genes the capacity to look the other way while aliens march past our sentries and eat our babies, for consideration. i am afraid some of us will always turn out to be gangsters with little thought of the consequences of a pernicious hunger for power and lucre. we purged the aphid patrol but did not educate our sisters about how to recognize compromise. we are all still at risk. maybe, someday, if we survive another million years, a greater capacity for hive intelligence will evolve in our genes. but for now, i fear that we may have missed an important teaching opportunity for the colony. we have also destroyed jobs in the aphid livestock enterprise which will have political consequences.

boss, there is a lesson here for you too.

factually reported and respectfully submitted as per agreement by cindi camponotus, official holly point farm investigative reporter and, by order of the queen, temporary special council and investigator into treasonous behavior.

Parasites

Editor's Notes: "Parasites" was first published in *The Broadkill Review*, April 1, 2021.

Further details on the money laundering operations of Semion Mogilevich, Sergey Kislyak, Michael Flynn, the Bratva gang, and other Russian mobsters can be found in *House of Trump, House of Putin: The Untold Story of Donald Trump and the Russian Mafia*, by Craig Unger, Dutton, 2018.

The Sarcophagidae is a family of flesh flies that practices kleptoparasitism as well as internal parasitism of other insects.

january 2019

the morning is hot. perspiration covers the barren ground. gray clay blotched with umber and burnt sienna is sanded with quartz grains. algae add random green and red accents. plants are small and sparse. it takes an ant like me several seconds to run from one to another, over and around dirt clods. i climb onto a daisy stem to look around. the sun shines green through my leaf shade. there are single clover plants. there are fuzzy rudbeckia dicots splashed with mud. there is a dried skeleton of mowed goose grass. blades of new bluestem and nut sedge emerge from the clay. the stage is bounded on three sides by an exposed tree root, a mulch pile, and a gravel road. at the edge of the mulch, several russula mushrooms grow. the red caps are scored with slug chewings. a broken mushroom cap is hollowed out by maggots. the tree root weeps sap—licked by a butterfly and two hornets. a checkered skipper uncoils its proboscis and sucks moisture from a damp spot. a female red velvet-assed cow killer, aka dasymutilla occidentalis, runs across the scene searching frantically. i stay hidden lest i fall victim to this termagant wasp.

holes the size of peas are scattered between plants one or two walking seconds apart. there are no excavation spoils surrounding these holes. they are naked. i see ten from my lookout.

i notice flies, lots of green-striped flies. the more i look, the more i see...dozens of them. they perch on plants and twigs close to the ground. their heads rotate as they watch with large black unblinking eyes. they are waiting...searching. they are flesh-eaters—from the sarcophagidae family. one lands next to me.

a oxybelus wasp with pale yellow rings around her abdomen enters, dragging a paralyzed fly impaled on her stinger shish-kebab fashion. she hauls it across the stage toward one of the holes. she gesticulates her antennae and moves to an adjacent hole. inspects it. she drags the fly in. she emerges a moment later and flies off.

my fly jumps up along with the others. they head for the wasp's hole. a kerfuffle ensues—a buzzing ball of bickering dipterids. when it disperses, i see a single fly emerge from the hole. it returns to my daisy. other flies land on twigs and dirt clods. i am surrounded. they are checking me out with their wraparound gangsta compound eyes. something seems sinister. my thorax hairs stand up. i need to find out what is going on here. i am not prepared for the story of disgusting depravity and deception i am about to hear.

the closest fly's gimballed head oscillates. i ask, 'hey, sister, who are you and what gives with the dipterid kerfuffle.'

the fly fixes me with seventeen thousand optical lenses and grumbles in a throaty russian accent, 'i am michelle flynnov-ich, special agent of f.s.b. we wait for fresh corpse. toss egg on it. wasp knows nothing. no raising kids for us. no ex-pense. no tuition. is free meal from stupid wasp. fly-babies hatch and eat whole corpse before wasp hatches. u.s. of a. is land of opportunity with sooo many stupid wasps digging holes and stocking with fresh corpses. is no crime. is no law from this. is capitalism. we kill you.'

i see where this gig is heading. i give the 'tripod salute' to alert the a.a.r.p. patrol—avian association for reciprocal pro-tection. three legs in the air signals possible distress, while a tripod plus waving tarsi—the 'thatcher'—calls in a strike. i stall for time.

'not so fast, sister,' i growl trying to sound like the law, 'you are talking to a 168-million-year veteran of intellectual evo-lution. all i see before me is a criminal band of sarcophage kleptocrats that toss their eggs on someone else's corpse. and i bet you don't pay your taxes either. what is this f.s.b.'

a second fly pipes up from the other side. 'f.s.b. is fly spy

41

bureau. is training for spreading disinformation, diphtheria, and depression in u.s. of a.'

'who are you,' i demand.

'semion sarcophage mogilevich, head of f.s.b. in charge of active measures. we are the bratva gang of flesh flies, little black face. corpse borrowing is okay but child kidnapping is favorite. i train tachinid parasite mob from brighton beach. fly maggot lies in path of young caterpillar. maggot drills into caterpillar, eats from inside. caterpillar feeds maggot. maggot chews way out, becomes fly. caterpillar dies. very efficient. no cages for children. no expense. no pesky lawyers. everybody happy...except caterpillar. is genius kompromat measure.'

flycatchers appear in the bushes overhead mixed with nervous, twitchy-tailed gnatcatchers. they hop from branch to branch nonchalantly pretending to glean. their nictitating eyes miss nothing of the scene below. the team is led by a great-crested flycatcher whose nom-de-guerre is tyrannus tyrannus.

i adopt a superior tone. 'okay, mister or mistress genius. you are spreading lies by flies, so where are the spies.'

semion sarcophage mogilevich insults me. 'little black-face ignorant bug. you never hear of 'fly-on-wall spy caper.' i invent. is genius. is called 'kislyak caper.' white house fly travel to white house in kislyak pocket. spy flies out and sits on wall. listen to orange leader. orange leader travel to dear leader with fly in pocket. fly listen. orange leader meets supreme russia leader with fly in pocket. fly jumps to supreme leader pocket. white housefly travel back to f.s.b. for debrief by huge horsefly with bare thorax. now we kill you.'

i get mad. 'you touch me and i tell the i.r.s. about your unpaid taxes, your illegal money, and your habit of sucking slimy scum from rotting carcasses.'

a highly aggravated semion sarcophage mogilevich shouts at me like i am some kind of foreigner. 'little bow-legged ant, we flick fly fertilizer at i.r.s. morons. if i.r.s. fall from tree, is too stupid to land on ground. f.s.b. has clean money. is coming by laundry bags. you investigate family business...now we really kill you.'

not wishing to press my luck to the lethal limit, i give the tripod and am in the middle of a tarsal thatcher when i hear the rising blurry 'quee-eeep' of tyrannus tyrannus. birds drop like bombs. wings beat as they level, lunge, and gulp flies. flies zip and buzz. dust rises. chitin is crunched. fly juice splatters me.

gnatcatchers' high-pitched war-whoops, zeee-beee, zeee-beee trill above the chaos. phoebes hover above, plucking escapees from the air. i am batted off my leaf by a gnatcatcher as he pulls out of a dive and crunches a fly where i stood. it is close combat. i manage to hang on with one leg and by the time i climb back up it is all over. fly legs and wings litter the battlefield. heads with wraparound eyes no longer oscillate and threaten. a few feathers float down. dust settles.

boss, the satisfaction i feel from this massive crunching of klepto-criminal necrophiles is diminished by the fact that there are so many kleptoparasites among us. never have so

Bird patrol decimates FSB kleptoparasites

many flies been so bereft of so many empathy genes. it was an evolutionary disaster that resulted in a mob of flies that treats butterfly caterpillars as nothing more than crawling meat lockers for personal gain. this would never happen in a eusocial ant community. with all your pernicious poisonous pesticides, is there anything you can do about this plague of flesh flies that will not destroy us all in the process. on further consideration, given your impotence and incompetence in dealing with parasites, maybe you should just look for the missing tax money.

factually reported and respectfully submitted as per agreement by cindi camponotus, official holly point farm investigative reporter

Cindi's Last Letter

february 2019

boss, this is my last letter. my old exoskeleton is wearing thin, and my tarsi ache from compressing your computer keys. i have outlived my genetic lifetime by a dozen ant-years. it is time for me to bid farewell to my colony, to you, my only friend among homo sapiens, and to all the insects that have educated, enriched, and entertained me. it has been a privilege bridging the gap between our species. i would like to reflect on my life, give you a hint about what you may expect from my successor, and offer you some worldly advice.

we both know i won't really die. i will live on for generations in the minds of all my fans who have read my reports, and have come to respect and admire me for my thoughts and philosophy. they will remember that i was a model student in spite of what it says on the colony walls. i never drank to excess nor beat up on my sisters. rumors to the contrary are the jealous natterings of political rivals.

ants will say, 'hey, remember that sarcastic little ant with all the big words. wow, i wish i could talk like that.' and then a drinking buddy—who is not blacked out or slobbering in his beer—will say, 'you could never talk like that, virgil. you are a

46

dumb-ass drone with no education. that ant was schooled— she probably went to m.i.t.' and then they will both have a good laugh and fall off their twigs. but the point will be made, boss. i will be remembered even in the primitive psyches of the daughters of the besotted ant confederacy.

folks will remember my heroism, boss, and maybe they will erect a statue in the colony commemorating the time i sallied forth on a suicide mission to rid your estate of pernicious wasps. a carving in rot-proof cypress with me brandishing a vorpal sword at a while-faced hornet would be nice. even though i really didn't do that, it is true in my dreams. and history can stand a little poetic license in the matter of a vorpal sword.

i know my finest hour will have mixed reviews. i am most proud of my job as special prosecutor when i arrested traitors in the colony and had them punished. it saved the colony from foreign inquilinists, literally. but i can hear the partisans now complaining in front of my statue, 'that bitch cindi is the one that arrested my aunt and had her torn apart and thrown on the compost heap. the deep-state queen gave her an award for it.' 'yeah, she should be locked up,' another snarls. 'lock her up,' they all shout.

as i leave this little paradise, i still do not comprehend your reaction to my essay on fake sex. i thought this was your favorite topic. Instead, it met with the enthusiasm of a painted lady in an orb weaver's web. i figured you would lap up the tale of the mega-narcissistic sex demon and the ice maiden like yellowjackets on rotten figs. how a diploid genome can be so obtuse in the mating game defies evolutionary logic.

why do you still exist.

i hope that my reports will outlast my corporal form so that my fans will think twice before referring to us as bugs or thinking of us as intellectually inferior or stepping on us. i ask you, as a matter of professional courtesy, to please not use my reports in your writing class or to garner emoluments that you do not turn over to the colony. my other reports have had a greater impact on you and your species. you have me to thank for investing your retirement funds in a nuclear submarine. i exposed foreign spies in your woods and extirpated a mob of sarco-parasites infesting your estate. i uncovered the techno-hemipteran source of hate speech on the planet. i am proud that some of my reports were published in your mainstream literary journals. have i advanced your benighted species' understanding of socio-biological-political truths. probably not.

this is not all about me. as you know, our queen makes quite a sperm collection on her first flight fling. this means that not all eggs are created equal, contrary to your homo notions about us. so, in accordance with my ancestors' house rules for these past forty homo sapiens years, i have chosen an egg of superior intellect, hatched it, and passed on my epigenetic traits such as electronic communications, antenna-internet interoperation, and journalistic integrity. of course, my apprentice will be called cindi. she knows how to operate your computer and will have her antennae tuned to the ethernet cable that runs underground past our colony. thank you for that convenience and the increased bandwidth. you are in good hands with cindi, boss.

this hasn't been easy. there is a lot of anger in this world. it is a challenge to teach a larva how to tap into the internet without her ending up as a smoldering fire ant. i hope she doesn't lose her objectivity and sense of humor. you will soon find out that my cindi has the self-righteous, passionate impatience of a young ant. i am leaving all my capital to the 'wee-too' foundation, which promotes 'insect dominance of the earth'—in.d.o.e. my apprentice is an in.d.o.e. community organizer. so watch yourself.

finally, a word of advice. i ask you to take the following suggestion in the spirit of friendship from an ant that no longer has a personal stake in the future of the planet but hopes her progeny will 'make the earth homo-less again.' you are over-populating the planet. stop it. it will cause the extinction of you and many of us with you. there have been several mass extinctions we ants have survived over the last 168 million years, but this next one will be the only one brought about by a single species. you don't have a gene that prevents the destruction of the planet—you have to consciously decide not to do this. instead, you have greed genes, which express unique and ugly homo sapiens traits.

boss, i bequeath you to my daughter. good luck. you will need it.

submitted with grace, humility, and hope, as per agreement by cindi camponotus, official holly point farm investigative reporter, deceased

A Short History of WEE-TOO

Editor's Note: "A Short History of WEE-TOO" was first published in *The Dead Mule School of Southern Literature*, March 2019.

spring 2019

i am disinclined to call you 'boss.' nobody is the boss of me. my stepmother said you could be manipulated by appealing to your male ego and your delusion of power derived from lethal pesticides. and if that didn't work, she said i was to eat a convincing piece of your house with the help of my half-million siblings. but she also said that if i didn't present a façade of political correctness and civility, my homo sapiens fan base would turn mean, call me a pest, and step on me like they are wont to do with all other insects. so i will flatter you with the 'boss' sobriquet for now in the interest of maintaining my stepmother's legacy readers. her fans are now my fans.

my fans are asking how an ant learned to manipulate computer keys and whether there are more ants doing keys. well, sirs and mesdames, i was raised by a stepmother, a cindi in a long line of cindis, who fed me on a high-protein, high-anti-oxidant and low-gluten diet which gave me super-ant powers and enabled me to be the spokes-ant for the colony. it is not just me who has more scientific knowledge than ten thousand college graduate homo sapiens. my sagacity is the product of individual contributions of an entire superorganism of a half-million ants. we evolved into a complex, adaptive euso-cial community with distributed intelligence. your computer scientists are just now realizing the power of distributed sys-tems with parallel processing. but you have not solved the conundrum of command and control that we ants mastered 168 million years ago. we are all autonomous agents bound together with shared meta-intelligence communicating via pheromones. you cannot even imagine it.

you have just become aware of the fact that homo sapiens is also a eusocial animal, which means you have division of labor and defend a common nest. i credit this self-awareness to your greatest natural philosopher, dr. edward osborne wil-son, who penned a biblical tome, *the ants*, which explained, for the first time, the superiority of the formicidae family over the homo genus and to whom you pay homage yourself, boss. your eusocial communities, however, are often dysfunctional, dishonest, and dangerous to the planet. i will comment more on this in later reports. for now, let me address the issue of computer keys. do my homo sapiens fans really think it is a big deal to poke at chicklets. really. this is not a big deal. so, boss, please tell them to get a life.

consider that we raise queens that lay over a thousand eggs a day for up to 30 years. that is a big deal. i'd like to see any one of your me-too mavens produce millions of offspring at the same time she manages a community of a half-million cooperating souls. go ahead, make it an olympic event and see who wins.

speaking of me-too, i need to inform you that ants created the whole concept of female solidarity millions of years ago. it is called 'wee-too,' which stands for 'women emancipated everywhere—together overwhelmingly omniscient.' it started 140 million years ago when ants, suffering from the arrogance of unfertilized males, decided they had enough. we called them hopeless, helpless haploids. before wee-too, our division of labor consisted of females who did all the work and males who carried sperm cells around—essentially six-legged gamete bags. males sat around and pretended to direct work. most of the time, all they did was watch sports, drink beer, smoke weeds, create monstrous messes, and fart. after which they would grab at us and force their vile-breathed, spasmodic attentions upon us. it was intolerable.

one hundred and twenty million years ago, female ants crafted the final solution. we were in charge of the nursery. we decided to out-breed nasty male predilections. we would genetically modify males into a drone caste. you are familiar with this process, boss, since you practice it on poultry, pigs, and politicians. sadly for us as a haplodiploidy species, if we got rid of the hapless males altogether, we would face genetic bankruptcy and fail to evolve. so we had to keep a minimum number of gamete carriers.

make no mistake. the perfection of a drone caste took millions of years. many alternatives were proposed. one was to breed males into dapper, dancing drones like bowerbirds.

Indolent drones before the WEE-TOO solution

your drone would dress for the occasion. when your drone got romantically inclined, he would build a trysting platform, dance on a branch, spin, flutter, spread his topknot, splay four legs, puff his chest, sing romantic love songs, twirl and jump and somersault, tell lewd jokes, recite sonnets, and exercise himself to exhaustion. this takes talent. his intended paramour watches, aloof, judging each jump and flip for height and originality, his costume for creativity, his copulatory stage for architectural excellence, and his love song for the passion and precision that titillates her little formicidae heart. these experiments were discontinued on account of hopeless haploid clumsiness. there was an utter lack of choreographic and architectural creativity among drones, except in cases when the males had same-sex tendencies, and that, of course, was no good to us.

another idea was to create super-courtiers that, in the manner of dragonflies, attach to a lover's neck and fly around having sex in midair, occasionally splashing one's paramour into a pond. this was dangerous to lives and limbs of women. unfortunately, the concept was revealed in the 'sad sack gamete news.' males lobbied hard for the idea. they formed a political action club called the 'craven-gnaws.' they would meet in a hackberry tree after the berries had dried and fermented. they would gnaw till they fell on the ground besotted, bloated, and blind. they had to be collected by the blotto patrol before stink bugs sucked out their vital bodily fluids. the craven-gnaws sued to get the 'dragonfly flutter'—their expression—adopted as a sanctioned sex scenario. lost in the politics was the fact that no male ant could lift a female off the ground and that scores of women had suffered broken necks in clinical trials mimicking dragonfly in-flight flagrante delicto.

the case made its way to the highest court, where the majority of the judges happened to be craven-gnaws. they were in the habit of meeting in secret to suck on forbidden fermented fruit. then they rendered anti-female decisions. the prospect of colony law sanctioning neck grabbing and dunking horrified the wee-too sisters. they decided that the craven-gnaws had to be impeached before the dragonfly flutter became law and ruined sex forever.

a band of wee-toos, taking 'impeachment' literally and having more enthusiasm than legal scholarship, kidnapped the craven-gnaw judges from their boozy backroom bunker and carried them to a peach tree. there they impaled the drunkards with greenbrier thorns and pinned them to twigs. these judges missed the court hearing. the case was decided by the unanimous opinion of the remaining all-female judges, who voted to save women from abusive sexual acts.

genetic modification experiments on males progressed for the next million years. eventually a model emerged that satisfied the wee-toos. it was called the 'drone-of-the-one-night-flight' and survives to this day as the evolutionary gold standard in haplodiploidy colonies. only a few drones are produced by this design. these get one chance at sex during the prospective queens' coming-out party. and then they die. if more than one queen makes it back to the hive, they battle it out till one queen rules them all. this event has become a huge spectator event driving employment in the summer doldrums.

once designed, it took only a hundred generations of selecting sensitive new-age males and discarding the excessively

hirsute to produce a civilized drone caste. the drones now revel in their identity. they created a new club of 'air force' drones with the motto, 'we fly high, have sex and die.' the 'drone-as-harmless-gamete-bag' was perfected.

the wee-too victory in the case of 'dragonfly flutter vs. wee-too' was the first in a long history of changes to our eusocial colony over the next twenty million years. after the impeachment, laws were passed that defined all males as a drone caste, abolished the craven-gnaw club, and limited the number of haploid drones that could be produced from unfertilized eggs. control of raising drone larvae was vested in the wee-too department for reproductive rights. then came laws against public drunkenness that required drones who fell out of trees to be thrown on the compost heap. after a few more million years, the drone education and civilization act passed, which required minimum training in sensitive new-age drone behavior and hygiene. this outlawed farting and scratching of private parts in public.

that is the history of wee-too. we are a proud sisterhood. we have the power. we control the nursery. we are the de facto and de jure majority. women have always done all the work and now have obtained our proportionate rewards. our history as eusocial ant colonies proves that when women take over political power, the results are stunningly successful. we are women emancipated everywhere, together overwhelmingly omniscient. we are wee-too.

boss, your friends of the female persuasion have a long way to go. they could use a history lesson on male gamete control. or maybe your females still empathize with your sad senescent state. maybe they believe homo sapiens males still have something useful to contribute to your evolution.

but here again, i flatter you.

submitted with grace, humility, and hope, as per agreement by cindi camponotus, official holly point farm investigative reporter and daughter of many past cindis

The Wall

Editor's Note: "The Wall" was first published in *The Dead Mule School of Southern Literature*, April 2020.

march 2019

1. the refugee

a pavement ant staggered into our guarded entrance the other day. she was waving a white flag and asking for asylum. we have never gotten an asylum seeker. strangers are usually eaten. the queen asked me to investigate. the refugee was shaking and agitated. i decided to hear her story.

first let me say that my recent reports have put me in the way of criticism on account of capitalization and punctuation. now that i am a published ant, i have no time for naive questions, so please explain to my fans that i can only push down one key at a time. folks shouldn't criticize what they can't understand.

i interviewed the officer in charge of immigrants at the colony gate.

cindi—'officer, how did this red ant sneak so close to our

entrance without becoming lunch.'

officer—'she was waving her t-shirt and asking for asylum or something. said she was the victim of the pink-faced persecution by prowling pernicious parasites. i don't know about asylums, ma'am, but she had some big words, so i arrested her and threw her in a cage. there are others like her staggering around at the border.'

i could see she was a tetramorium—a class of hairy red ant given to flightiness, low intellect, and loose morals. i am a broad-minded ant but am wary of redheads running drugs into our colony or worse. they could pollute our genetic purity. they may copulate with our dimwitted drones and produce some kind of purple queen.

Tetramorium immigrans ants

cindi—'why come all the way from the pavement asking us for asylum.'

cinder—'your honor, ma'am, my name is cinder. i am a tetramorium from the sidewalk.' she became hysterical and started screaming, 'help...the raiders are coming...the raiders are coming... get out now.'

cindi—'calm down, pet. tell us your story.'

cinder—'we began to have visitors. they were pink-faced and kind of skin-headed. they lurked, taking notes. they said they were tourists. more and more sisters didn't return from foraging. we got suspicious. the pinkfaces spoke our language with accents. like, 've vill give to you yobs, yes. many, many yobs. so many good yobs. ve vill make eu safe egin. oh, so many vonderful, vonderful yobs.' it sounded like they had a labor shortage wherever they came from and were recruiting us.'

cindi—'so you have tourists with foreign accents promising jobs. didn't that make you suspicious.'

cinder—'more than that. after a few sisters limped in—beat up and bleeding—the mystery of the pesky pinkfaces and disappearing sisters made it to the queen. the sisters had been abducted and put into brain-reprogramming by pinkfaces. they were being made into slaves and worked until they died.'

cindi—'didn't it occur to you that these pink-faced tourists may be members of the strongylognathus clan of slave raiders.'

cinder—'not then. but the queen believed that they were up to no good. she called them all kinds of names, like 'social parasites' and 'deplorable despicable dishonest deadbeats'. she told us to stop all pinkfaces at the border and to build a wall around our colony. the wall had to be vertical and topped with greenbriar thorns. it had to have slots made from twigs so we could shoot venom between them. it had to be as high as a pubescent mugwort. our soldiers argued that no ant colony was ever protected by a wall. and that ants can climb vertical surfaces. but then rumors spread, and more and more workers became convinced that the slave raiders were coming to spread disease and psychedelic drugs.'

cindi—'did you build a wall in spite of your military's objections.'

cinder—'yes. it was impossible to resist. spontaneous demonstrations popped up. ants were chanting, 'build the wall, build the wall, build the wall.' more and more sisters were abducted even as they worked on the wall. the queen couldn't resist the populist panic. she had no alternative. she was afraid she would be torn apart by a mob of fearmongers. the wall was almost completed when i got abducted by a pinkface wearing a red hat. i escaped by squirting formic acid at her pink face which blew off her hat and confused her. ma'am, they are coming for us and they will come for you too. i know it. you need to run now… or build a wall… or raise an army and attack… or do something.'

2. the wall

cindi—'okay, okay,' i said, 'let's see this wall and reconnoiter the situation.' i convinced our terrorized refugee to lead me to a bush overhanging her colony. i was curious. i had never seen an ant-wall. from our lookout we beheld tetramorium-ville surrounded by a wall with crenellations and sentry posts. thorns stuck up along the top. hairy red ants patrolled the battlements. their abdomens bulging with formic acid. it was like a scene from your macbeth, boss—a castle in the scottish highlands surrounded by a fortified wall. the surrounding green meadows waved rhythmically.

'yikes,' i exclaimed.

the meadow was marching to tetramoriumville, but this was not a real meadow. we were witnessing the attack of the slave raiders. the soulless, slave-making strongylognathus raiders were marching rank upon rank in platoons and battalions. thousands of pale pink ants holding blades of grass vertically in their mandibles were advancing like a tide of green across the pavement. It was mesmerizing and stomach-churning. we were terrified. i regurgitated lunch. we froze to our overhanging branch.

they surrounded the wall. strongylognathus attackers started climbing up to us. we crept up higher. the raiders only went high enough to hang over the colony and drop down into it. on the ground, the slavers threw down their grass in front of the wall and climbed up and over, ignoring the sprays of formic acid from the defenders, who couldn't fit their abdomens through the slats and direct their spray sideways. pinkfaces sprayed the colony with copious amounts of highly concentrated alarm pheromones. the colony erupted in panic. there was pandemonium among the tetramorium. the defenders rushed to the opposite wall and piled up against it.

strongylognathus soldiers waded in and carried off my refugee's sisters. those that resisted were held down and torn
apart by slavers. all the time, the slave raiders were shriek-
ing, 'lock them up. lock them up. lock them up...'

a few tetramorium ants managed to make it over the wall, but
most of these were kidnapped by strongylognathus raiders
and hauled away.

boss, i have never seen such a feckless defense. weaponized fake pheromones spread such confusion that the defense was impotent, incompetent, and ineffectual. there was
nothing for us to do, hanging on as we were, overhead in the
bushes. it was a sad, sad scene. we were one carpenter ant
and a tetramorium refugee against an army of strongylognathus slave raiders. we returned to my colony.

3. the rebellion

i reported to our queen. she was appalled and upset lest the
same thing happen to us. she tasked me with an additional
mission that was far more dangerous. i was commanded to
lead a small party of wee-too sisters to the strongylognathus stronghold and mount a counterintelligence operation
that would destroy it and exterminate slave raiders in the
neighborhood.

you remember, boss, that 'wee-too' means 'women emancipated everywhere—together overwhelmingly omniscient.'
in an earlier report, i explained how the wee-too movement
evolved over millions of years as colony sisters developed the
courage and laid down the legal and evolutionary foundation
to liberate formicidae females from hopeless haploid drones.

this made our eusocial community great again.

i assembled a tiger team of wee-toos. we were black-faced. we travelled by night to blend in. within sight of the strongy-lognathus stronghold, we went incognito with pink face and pink body suits. we mugged a few dozen sentries, tied them into pretzels, and stole their red hats. we wore rose-colored sunglasses.

we penetrated to the reprogramming chamber. there we be-held row upon row of captive tetramorium ants in the thrall of a single strongylognathus 'slave master' wearing a huge red hat, who bellowed phrases into a loudspeaker. these were followed up by a dispirited loud groan from the ranks, like this:

master—'clean latrine'

slaves—'yes ma'am, yes ma'am'

master—'stash the trash'

slaves—'yes ma'am, yes ma'am'

master—'want some food, don't be rude'

slaves—'yes ma'am, yes ma'am'

master—'punch out protest'

slaves—'yes ma'am, yes ma'am'

master—'cage the children'

slaves—'yes ma'am, yes ma'am'

master—'lock her up'

slaves—'lock her up. lock her up. lock her up.'

it went on and on until the slaves fell into a rhythmic trance. they milled about in little circles. there was a strong smell of fake pheromone permeating the chamber. we left before we puked. our squad spread out. no red-hats were doing any work. it appeared that they didn't know how. they just stood around and watched with baleful, puckered mandibles while the slaves self-organized into work crews that did everything from cleaning to tending the queen to bringing in forage. they fed all the larvae, many of which were tetramorium captives who were destined to be brainwashed.

we reassembled. our plan was to use the strongylognathus' own apartheid system to destroy them. we sprang into action. we accosted a dozen tetramoriums that still had some light in their eyes and convinced them they could escape if they stuck together. we brought tiny bags of strange-smelling pheromone with us unlike anything you could smell in the strongylognathus colony so it would be ignored by the red-hats. strapping the bags to their abdomens, wee-too sisters led our first escapees to a safe hole far away in the pavement. the scent trail was strengthened by each new escapee. they blazed a private perfumed path to freedom. the rest of us continued to recruit tetramoriums and send them along the scented trail. red-hats thought their slaves were just going out to forage. but the emancipated tetramoriums never returned.

after a few days, we had a constant trickle of asylum seek-ers. the colony had visibly shrunk. the tetramoriums sang as they marched out of apartheid and followed the freedom pheromone.

singing freedom marchers: 'follow the freedom scent. follow the freedom scent. all god's insects gonna march away to freedom when they follow the freedom scent.'

tetramorium sisters heard the singing and slunk off to join the march. the tenuous trickle became a refugee river. we no longer had to recruit—which was good because we ran out of freedom pheromone sacks. our squad of wee-toos watched from an overhanging bush as former slaves abandoned their jobs and crept away. soon all we saw were groups of red-hats wandering around aimlessly. they were starving. by the time they realized that their labor force had absconded, it was too late. they had no energy to give chase. starvation was made worse because the last of the tetramoriums emptied the storerooms—they believed they were going on a picnic. the next day, the few strongylognathus still alive were collapsed on their backs groaning, 'i am so hungry, feed me, feed me.'

we gathered up as many red-hats from the dying colony as our squad could carry and headed for home. passing by the emancipated tetramoriums, we noticed they were hard at work creating a new queen. they would be okay...for a while.

4. the alliance

boss, our counterintelligence operation against the strongy-lognathus was perhaps the most effective implementation of active measures ever. we exterminated an entire colony of inquilinists who never knew what hit them until it was too late. but our work wasn't done. the queen wanted to guarantee that our colony would never fall prey to inquilinist spies who would pour into our community and attack us with fake pheromones. we needed a preemptive offense. we needed higher powers. we needed powerful allies. we needed... diplomacy.

the trick to diplomacy is to get different species to cooperate, because it is in their self-interest to do so, without one party being eaten by the other. it is called symbiosis and is more common among animals and plants than your scientists can ever imagine. the queen commanded me to create a symbiosis that would rid our country of all species of slave raiders.

i went in search of the notorious 'ant-bane,' aka colaptes auratus, to see if we could strike a deal. this was dangerous. northern flickers eat ants all day long. i hid behind a leaf at his roost and spoke to him with my gravelly, disembodied man-voice. it is a favorite trick of mine. when folks hear a voice in the woods, they assume it is god talking. we worked out a deal in which his flock would look for a circle of red-hats in the grass. in the middle of the target he would find a colony of tasty strongylognathus which they would tear apart and then feast on the inhabitants. in return for this highly specific market research, he was to stay away from the environs of the persimmon tree wherein we reside.

this is working. we have extirpated all species of slave raiders within a week's march. That is as far as we can march carrying all those red-hats. boss, i may ask you for a ride on the golf cart so we can extend our geobiological hegemony

The deal to end slavery

to parts unknown. let me know if you want to join this symbiotic community. there may be something in it for you in the way of greater lepidopteran chrysalis survivorship if we protect them from parasitic ichneumon wasps. you decide. being so smart, you probably don't have anything as stupid as a bunch of red-hatted homo sapiens carrying children off to cages or brainwashing your neighbors with indoctrination chants. but if you should chance upon this, i suggest a dose of diplomacy. because it appears that walls are an evolutionary dead end.

factually reported and respectfully submitted as per agreement by cindi camponotus, official holly point farm investigative reporter

The Doomed

april 2019

a chicken wandered through the woods the other day mumbling to herself. distracted, she shambled back and forth across the path dragging her wings, depressed and exhausted. fearing the worst—an outbreak of bird flu—i spoke to her from the underside of an ilex sapling.

'yo, chicken little,' i hailed, 'pipe up and give us a tune.' at this the itinerant chicken looked around. finding no immediate audience, she straightened up, stuck her pruned beak in the air, and turned up the volume:

'we're downhearted, depressed, and doomed,
rolling through here today,
headed for jobs at a chick-fil-a,
in a curious, roundabout way.

life was cozy, nestled in eggs,
but when we hatched,
we were grabbed by the legs,
and took our last ride in a cramped little cage.

"We're downhearted, depressed, and doomed"

we were lied to and tricked,
our suspicions aroused,
all so that humans
could eat fewer cows.

as we bounced along in that truck of sighs,
too late for a will and useless to cry,
the wisest among us have come to realize
that the people who eat us are doomed likewise.

at the end of the day,
humans will pay.
global warming
is coming your way!'

seeing her beak was whacked off, i felt safe enough to climb out on top of my prickly leaf and converse compound eye to nictitating eyeball. i interrupted before my feathered ac-quaintance went suicidal. 'avast, my bitter little blunt-nose, what's with the doom and gloom.'

'i blew out the back of an eighteen-wheeler and landed in a drainage ditch,' she said. 'any feed grain around here.'

'only ticks and chiggers,' i said, 'but why are poultry-eaters doomed.'

my depressed poult whimpered, 'they fill us with hormones and antibiotics. we pay them forward. and if that doesn't kill off chicken-eaters, global warming will. as the last chicken-truck-of sighs stalls on the road with an exploding radiator in one-hundred-and-forty-degree heat, we will be laughing our feathered asses off. humans did this to us. you fried, broiled, and fricasseed us. now you are doing it to yourselves. ha ha ha ha ha...sigh.'

she shambled off down the path.

boss, you are outnumbered by chickens in this county five thousand one hundred and forty to one.

think about it.

factually reported and respectfully submitted as per agreement by cindi camponotus, official holly point farm investigative reporter

Pâté de Fois

Editor's Note: Cindi accompanied us to the south of France in 2019. Her French is "American Tourist."

bordeaux, june 2019

boss, you're going to get us excommunicated from france. quit sending pâté de foie back to the kitchen. that was a michelin star restaurant you insulted this evening. the kitchen roaches, sporting stove-pipe chapeaux and paring knives, almost guillotined me.

they railed, 'zut, vos américains sont vraiment sans classe, très stupide, et totalement gauche. c'est horrible.'

i had to renounce your pedestrian taste and confess to your lack of culture, your utter savagery, and swear that i, indeed, loved goose liver. 'oui mes chers camarades, ils n'ont pas de culture alimentaire. mais moi, j'aime beaucoup le pâté de foie d'oie.'

after i recanted for you, the fat kitchen roaches began stuffing me with your leftovers, trying to kill me with goose pâté. it wasn't bad tasting. less lean than your well-exercised ground beetle paste and less pungent than grasshopper pâté, which,

They stuffed me with pâté de fois

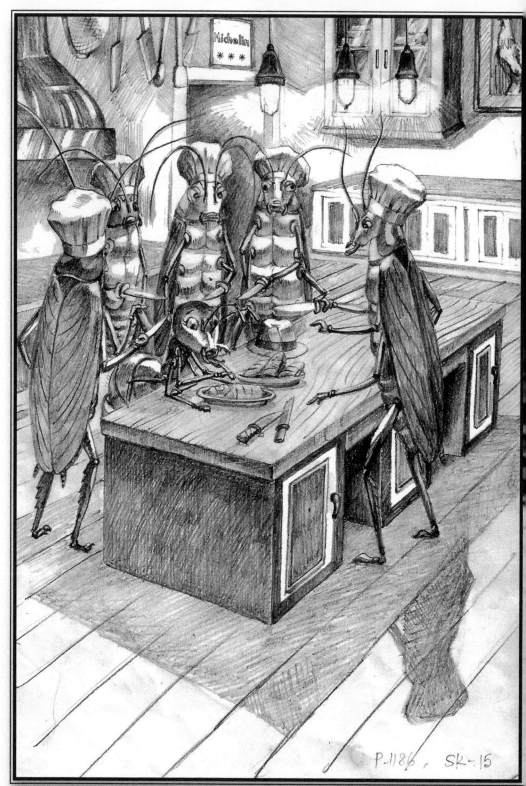

i explained, 'c'est mieux que le foie sauterelle.'

that appeased them so i was able to stumble out of there before my arteries totally clogged up.

in the future, i suggest you adopt a more cosmopolitan attitude regarding foreign cuisine, boss. ingesting a pesticide-soaked liver pâté once in a great while won't kill you, immediately. insects do that all the time. it is about time you found out what that is like.

respectfully submitted as per agreement by cindi camponotus, official picardi expedition scribe on assignment in bordeaux, france

Yellowjackets

bordeaux, june 2019

the yellowjackets around bordeaux have major attitudes. They are not your friendly picnic wasps that just want to share your lemonade. they call themselves les 'gilet jaunes.' i call them the jilly jawns, which is the american patois. they swarm at traffic circles, which the french use instead of traffic lights since they add danger to otherwise boring intersections. i spoke to a partisan wearing a beret and a pointed goatee. he looked more like a depressed impressionist than a picnic wasp. i mustered up my best argot. 'mouseer, pourquoi le démonstration.'

'mon petite bête,' he responded, 'nous faisons la révolution pour la liberté, l'égalité, et la fraternité.'

nice slogan. i pushed for specifics. 'ce sont de belles paroles, mouseer, mais que vooly-voo exactly.'

'ma fourmi bourgeois,' he replied, 'nous exigeons d'abord, arbres avec des fruits pourris dans tous les parcs, deuxièmement la fin des pesticides et troisième, un nid de gilet jaune sur chaque maison,'

"We want our rights and we don't care how"

i expressed doubt that they could even get the french government to plant trees with rotten fruit in every park much less to ban pesticides so that their tribe could build nests on every house in france.

he lowered his head and focused three thousand of his eye lenses on me, like i was a pitiful wretch. he claimed that the jilly jawns were descended from napoleon's bees, which were and still are an omnipresent and powerful political force. he said these bees are woven into the fabric of tapestries, painted on masterpieces, and stamped on millions of bars of soap sold to tourists.

'my dear jilly jawn,' i replied, 'vous êtes trompé avec de fausses nouvelles.' i told him that besides being fooled with fake news, he was no more descended from a napoleonic honeybee than i am descended from a religiously devout praying mantis. i observed that the french treat the descendants of napoleon's bees as aristocracy while the jilly jawns get the bug bomb.

he took umbrage at this and called me a cowardly beast. 'vous êtes une bête lâche.' gesticulating wildly with four legs, he proceeded to explain that i deserved to be stomped on like an ant because i was too cowardly to swarm up inside a gendarme's flak jacket and puncture his private parts. he buzzed off shouting that they wanted their rights and they didn't care how. 'nous voulons nos droits et nous ne nous soucions pas comment. toujours gaie.'

i don't doubt that if these populist jilly jawns could rally enough comrades to swarm a large fraction of the gendarmerie at once, it would sting politically. but boss, what would be the message in that. that picnic wasps are pissed off... then what, rotten fruit in parks. more likely pesticides to put down the rebellion. and after that, what, another napoleon.

respectfully submitted as per agreement by cindi camponotus, official picardi expedition scribe on assignment in bordeaux, france

Bonaparte's Revenge

bordeaux, june 2019

i met one of napoleon's roosters in a bordeaux park today. he walks around with an 'attitude nonchalante' picking up crumbs around picnic tables by the monument to dead revolutionary soldiers. he doesn't catch the occasional tossed crust. he leaves them to a local flea-bitten chien. if the crumb is too small, he sticks up his nose, and the french-speaking english sparrows get it. he struts with a pomposity that suits his elaborate uniform. he wears a tail of luxuriously weeping dark green plumes. his face, crest, and wattles are blood orange. he is feathered in various shades of orange on his rump to red, crimson, and burgundy on his chest with a dignified touch of gray on his nape.

i would call his outfit 'pre-revolutionary louis quatorze.' we had a conversation.

cindi—'avast, regal one. how goes the begging business.'

rooster—'not begging. je suis appelé bonaparte, 'le coq qui chant'. bonaparte ne beg pas. je suis capitaine du corps des coqs dans le grande armée de la république. capitaine bonaparte rallies troops et chant battle song pour glorious

Bonaparte, 'le coq qui chant.'

revolution. nous chantons la nouvelle marseillaise. c'est merveilleux.'

s'il vous plait, movez vous de cette croissant crust, ma petite bête, je suis vegan... et comment vous appelez-vous.'

i appreciated that hint as the croissant crust disintegrated under the staccato attack of his republican beak.

cindi—'enchanté to meet you, mon capitaine. i am called cindi, the erudite ant. i am descended from one hundred million generations of bourgeoise carpenters who toiled in the american colonies long before the concept of freedom was invented and long before citizens had the audacity to revolt against their queen.'

bonaparte—'you counterrevolutionary royalist beast. i peck your queen-loving ass to shreds.'

cindi—'not so fast, mon capitaine of coqs. vous savez... je suis un américain. nous sommes des allies. shredding my butt will be an international incident. it will be coq au vin for you.'

i try to distract him before he reverts to an insectivore. 'alors, mon capitaine, chant us a little revolutionary ditty. inspire the troops to wreak bloody hell on the tyrannical ancien régime.'

bonaparte—'ah, ma petite cindi, je suis le coq qui chant. j'ai créé le nouveau rap de la résistance. bien écouter.'

thus inspired to belt out his new creation, the 'rap of the resistance,' he flutters onto a picnic table and begins scratching. he lets out a series of 'cock-a-doodle-doos' that attract the attention of a dozen tourists. they turn to see the cause of ear-splitting crowing, which is loud enough to wake up the revolutionary soldiers who are entombed nearby. the tourists take out their cell phones and begin the selfie ritual. i take shelter under a crumbled pastry wrapper stuck to the end of the table with cherry filling. things will get interesting...and maybe dangerous.

bonaparte begins to scratch and ruffle his photogenic feathers. he crows to the crowd. I have translated most of his rap.

bonaparte—

    'vive la liberté et vive la france.
    i'm bonaparte le coq with a patriotic dance.
    toujours gaie and cock-a-doodle-doo,
    join us in the dance or end up in the stew.

    rich class clings to hereditary wealth.
    madame la guillotine is a hazard to their health.
    allons enfants de la patrie,
    contre nous de la tyrannie.

    join the bloody fight for wage equality,
    or the oligarchs will cook you into chicken fricassee.
    toujours gaie and cock-a-doodle-doo,
    join us in the dance or end up in the stew.

    they will masticate your livers and serve you on a toast.
    they will baste you with their fake news and cook you as
    a roast.
    they will fill you full of lies and things you never knew,
    and tell you it's a privilege to be baked as cordon bleu.

    toujours gaie and cock-a-doodle-doo,
    join us in the dance or end up in the stew.'

now the crowd is swinging to the scratching rhythm, and
bonaparte is a red-orange blur. dust rises. they all cock-a-
doodle-doo at the choruses. energy increases. they chant
over and over.

'toujours gaie and cock-a-doodle-doo,
join us in the dance or end up in the stew.'

bonaparte soaks up the energy. he shreds the picnic table. sawdust flies. he does flips, flapping his wings and crowing after each chorus. feathers float. the crowd eggs him on. they chant the chorus to get him to flip for their selfies. i sense they were more into the media than the message. the scene is intense.

'toujours gaie and cock-a-doodle-doo,
join us in the dance or end up in the stew.'

i have to escape before someone crumples up my pastry wrapper and throws me in the trash. or bonaparte, the republican rooster, forgets he is vegan and gobbles me up like a reactionary fascist at a freedom fest. there are too many stomping feet, so i hang on underneath the thumping table. i only remember a few more verses before my brain gets scrambled from the dusty screaming kerfuffle.

'rally, all you chickens, to the noble cause.
we are marching under torchlights.
we are changing all the laws.

toujours gaie and cock-a-doodle-doo,
join us in the dance or end up in the stew.

we are chasing out the foreigners.
we'll have chicken purity.
we will only have our freedom
when all chickens look like me.

toujours gaie and cock-a-doodle-doo,
join us in the dance or end up in the stew.

politicians are disgusting.
our leaders are corrupt.
bring guns and ammunition.
let your righteous bile erupt.

toujours gaie and cock-a-doodle-doo,
join us in the dance or end up in the stew.

we are the revolution.
we are bringing on a flood.
the streets will turn to crimson
with the ruling class's blood.

toujours gaie and cock-a-doodle-doo,
join us in the dance or end up in the stew.'

it goes on until bonaparte collapses into an orange heap of feathers with a blood-red face. his new rap is in the genre of the original marseillaise. he updated it since they now have politicians instead of real kings to behead. it appeals to a crowd...especially chickens who feel cheated and afraid of the pot. when we get home, boss, look out for coqs crowing from picnic tables. it riles up the chickens. they have a tendency to revolt against the ruling class when they think their future is coq au vin, with no wine in advance. back in the day, it got bloody in france.

we have a lot of chickens back home. it could get ugly on the farm.

factually reported and respectfully submitted as per agreement by cindi camponotus, official picardi expedition scribe
on assignment in bordeaux, france

The Neon Skink

september 2019

i met a skink in the garage. he was a toothy plestiodon fascia-tus. his kind has been leaving calling cards of the scatological kind in the garage all summer.

i called from behind the roundup jug, 'yo, your fasciatusness, what brings your tribe here in such abundance.'

he licked his toothy chops and slurred out a response, as lizards with sticky tongues are wont to do. 'schtep out here, litthle morthal, and i will thplain it all.'

i threatened, 'avast, lizard dude. i am all slathered in round-up here. if you violate my civil rights, pernicious cancerous polyps will pop out of your skinky skin. you will be as dead as a green fly on the business end of a swatter and twice as fast.' i stepped out into the light. 'why are you here—are you political, economic, environmental, or terrorism refugees, or are you simply bereft of birth control.'

'my litthle philothophical bug,' he replied in a condescend-ing tone, 'we thrive becauth of the absenthe of jays, cuckoos, and hawths, becauth of the abundanth of pill bugs, becauth the winters are warming, becauth there are no caths around, and becauth we believe in the thanctity of the reptile egg. our purpothe is to prolitherate on t'earth.'

'see here, loquacious lizard,' i replied, 'i don't mean to be mean or excessively mundane, but the oligarch that owns this garage takes a dim view of lizard poop. there are rules and norms of behavior here. like 'treat this house with re- spect and don't eat it or poop in it,' and in return, nobody gets pesticided.'

he reared up on his forelegs and stretched his neck. 'rulths. i sthpit on your rulths. i do what i want and everybody geths outta my way. you don't like my rulths, thew me. yes, thew me,' he slurred.

in my patient tone, as if toilet training an emergent ant, 'my dear fasciatus, there are rules and laws you have to respect. like the laws of nature and the universe. one is that if you poop in the garage, you will be held to account. there will be consequences.'

mr. fasciatus turned bright neon and got belligerent. 'oh black-faced ignorant inthect... you are justh inferior. you don't have backbones or shiny blue tails. thstop telling me how to live and go back to your filthy mouth-infested ant hole where you came from.'

his racial slurs inspired my superior response 'i will not de- bate the merits of your class versus the insect class except to say that we were here long before you and will be here long after. you may think you are above the law, but some day when you are strolling in the sun, singing a lizard lullaby, you will reap the consequence of your arrogance and anti-insectivism.' just then, i looked out of the garage, and 9,800 of my optical lenses spied a blue jay in the sweet gum tree looking over the driveway.

mine were the last words heard by the pompous skink. 'so mr. fasciatus, i bid you goodbye with a prediction that your disregard for rules of behavior and natural laws will be your undoing.'

his last words to me, 'ah, like we don't eat your kind for lunch all day long. watch me.'

with that, the lizard with the neon tail and matching ego strolled out onto the gravel drive, lurching from stone to stone, occasionally lapping up a stink bug or a sarcophagid fly. all the time he hummed his lizard lullaby.

'i do what i wanna do.
don't like it, you can just thew.
do wacka do wacka shiny tailths rule.

don't care 'bout all your rulths.
laws are for the rest 'o you fools.
do wacka do wacka shiny tailths rule.

i crawled up the wall to get a better view. to the jay, the neon tail in the sunlight flashed 'eat me.' the jay dropped like a stone, spread its wings just before it hit the gravel, and pierced mr. fasciatus through his back with a perfectly practiced puncture punch. mr. jay flew back to his perch and proceeded to flail the once-proud lizard against the branch to tenderize the lizard's uninformed and reckless views concerning natural laws and the rules of survival.

"Do wacka do wacka, shiny tails rule."

i didn't hang around for the dismemberment. I raced back home to alert my nestmates that there may be lizard parts dropping from heaven.

too bad for mr. fasciatus. he didn't survive to pass his newly acquired wisdom on to the next generation. but then if lizards like him learned the rules, then what would jays do for protein.

boss, you can make all the rules you want about where civilized creatures poop. but at the end of the day, if certain classes don't respect the rule of law, what are your options. it would be easy for me to round up a flock of jays and have them lap up lawless lizards. but what are you going to do about your homo sapiens 'lizard fasciatuses.'

factually reported and respectfully submitted as per agreement by cindi camponotus, official holly point farm investigative reporter

Epitaph for Humanity

october 2019

i have been waiting to write this epitaph for homo sapiens my entire life. it appears your extirpation has just begun in earnest and i don't want your news organizations to scoop me. i can't wait another year for my apprentice to take up my crusade because she might miss something. i have lived through these last few years of moral and ecological angst and she has not.

the last few years have been the morning of the evening of homo sapiens. sad for you but happy for all other species. so boss, i dedicate this extinction poem to you in thanks for bequeathing your farm to us. actually, it was ours all along.

homo sapiens had a short run.
compared to others, its reign just begun.
you should have survived at least as long
as the primate group to which you belong.

you got off to a running start,
with sweating skin and a thumping heart,
until running made an offensive smell,
and your lazy heart became unwell.

with ability to organize,
you killed game of larger size.
then stealing from another tribe
led to war and genocide.

your agile and predicting brain
spawned companies which were your bane.
they metastasized, like gods behaved,
and made homo sapiens their slave.

you created arts of every kind,
architecting structures, which you left behind.
then you imagined the divine,
which caused suffering and more genocide.

your science, based on thought empirical,
cured human plagues like a miracle.
for human needs, the science solution
sated wants and spewed pollution.

like a continent-sized meteor, you burst upon the scene,
an intelligent ape with no stewardship gene.
with all your smarts you should have foreseen
this sixth extinction in the anthropocene.

in the cretaceous extinction that came before,
seventy-six percent vanished, but you'll waste even more.
most of the birds and fish in the sea,
and millions of insects that you've never seen.

with micro-plastics, acid waves, fires and storms,
you're no longer here but your deeds changed the norms.
your legacy lives for all that survive—
their genes had to change in order to thrive.

you tragically failed throughout history
to show your brothers enough empathy,
to help humans in other geographies,
beyond where your leader's self-interest might be.

over billions of years, life from the past
was sequestered in carbon, which you burned too fast.
in three hundred years you released so much heat
that from run-away swelter, there was no retreat.

one fact of your time that is really sad,
compared to the life a few of you had,
most of your kind lived in abject subsistence.
very few would have said it was a nice existence.

your intelligence was your unique specialty,
but you failed to adapt to earth's reality.
in the rocks below your plastics persist.
by all other creatures you won't be missed.

with no people around, there'll be no history,
so, the passing of humans won't be a mystery.
no one will know you were ever there.
surviving life forms will not even care.

boss, i am getting old and my exoskeleton creaks and aches. i
will soon join my predecessors in the chitinous carcass crypt.

my replacement, whose nom de guerre is also cindi, will do a laudable job of reporting farm-wide foibles. as you swelter in the heat and battle rising seas, please remember—you heard it here first.

factually reported and respectfully submitted as per agreement by cindi camponotus, official holly point farm investigative reporter

Ants Lead Global
Conspiracy to Take
Back the Earth

Editor's Note: I found the fully formatted article, "Ants Lead Global Conspiracy to Take Back the Earth," on my computer. It was intended for publication in the *New York Times* "Science" section in April 2020. I comment here on its provenance and possible motivation.

That it never appeared in the *Times* science section is probably a blessing because it would have caused a scandal which would have embroiled me in an international kerfuffle. I suspect the report was written by Cindi Camponotus for the science section of the *Times* and sent to them for formatting and editing, outside of the usual arrangement that Cindi and I have worked under for the last five years. The *Times* then sent the draft back and began to verify references and quoted sources. Unable to locate either Dr. Lepidoptera or Cindi, the *Times* editors dropped the story. And Cindi left it on the screen for some reason.

Before I delve into Cindi's motivation and the implications of the report, I must express my admiration for Cindi's indirection by her fabrication of a scientist author. This is evidence of strategic thinking at a level that supersedes the factual reporting she has been doing. This fabrication gives the report the credibility of a credentialed scientist author as opposed to the rantings of a random ant.

As to Cindi's motivation, I can think of several possibilities. First, the whole story of a conspiracy among Formicidae tribes to exterminate the human species is fake news. Cindi is using misdirection to send scientists off on a wild goose chase which will delay finding and dealing with the COVID-19 disease. The misdirection may buy ants some respect on the world stage for a while. They may be recognized as a worthy adversary by a species that respects others who visit violence against their adversaries.

Under the assumption that the report is true and only the author's name is faked, the situation is more complex. Two possibilities present. One is that Cindi knows of the conspiracy and *deliberately* left the report on my computer as a warning to me personally of things to come. This would imply she views us as more than business associates—maybe we are *friends.* That our relationship is more than a transactional symbiosis and includes a modicum of empathy would imply a whole new dimension of Cindi's personality. for Cindi—she may be a being with emotions. Animal behaviorists are finding more and more evidence that non-human animals, indeed, have emotions.

The last possibility is that Cindi knows of the conspiracy, and my discovery of the report was accidental—she forgot to erase it. This implies a level of subterfuge on her part of which I did not know she was capable. It is well-known among animal behaviorists that more and more animals can simulate outcomes and choose their behavior to benefit themselves. Given Cindi's clear resentment of humanity's treatment of the environment, and insects in particular, and in light of her full-throated indictment of Homo sapiens in "Epitaph for Humanity," this seems to me the most likely possibility.

If the report is true, I find it entirely credible that the research is being led by the fire ant clan. By their aggressive personalities they have ignited a smoldering war between themselves and humanity, which could now be entering a more lethal phase. I note also that the likelihood of ant clans communicating common grievances among themselves and then banding together in a pan-Formicidae confederacy is much more likely than any one species establishing communication between themselves and a human. Some communities of ants that share the same genome can span hundreds of miles.

Chemical-biological weaponry is widespread among animals and plants. Humans have been developing biological weapons for generations. Symbiotic relationships between ants and microbes have been well documented. Most herbivorous insects synthesize antidotes for the many toxins produced by plants. Is it too much to expect that highly developed eusocial species could develop microbial defensive weapons?

Finally, while this is the only evidence of such a conspiracy I have found, that does not mean it is over or that it is not ongoing. Antipathy toward Homo sapiens may be more widely shared up and down more taxa of animals, and even plants, than humans could ever imagine. I suggest the reader approach Cindi's next report on a Formicidae conspiracy with some skepticism, less humor, and more credibility than her previous missives.

Anthony Picardi

SCIENCE

CLIMATE | SPACE & COSMOS | HEALTH | TRILOBITES | SCIENCETAKE | EVOLUTION | OUT THERE

Ants Lead Global Conspiracy
to Take Back the Earth
Entomologist describes super-exponential disease spread caused by symbiosis between a virus and a Formicidae superorganism
Did political chaos thwart the plan to exterminate Homo sapiens?

By Dr. Antoine Lepidoptera
April 9, 2020

Updated 12:15 p.m. ET

ACCOMACK COUNTY, VA—Epidemiologists are at a loss to explain the origins of the unique coronavirus, COVID-19, now surging in the United States. Early claims that infections originated with travelers from China have been superseded by new DNA evidence showing that the first infections arrived with travelers from Europe. Epidemiologists are still baffled, however, by the rapid and simultaneous spread of the virus in all corners of the globe. Now evidence has emerged that the virus may not have spread on its own. The spread of COVID-19 appears to have been accelerated by non-microbial organisms which have used the unwitting virus to launch a pernicious political plot against the human species.

The first hints that other biological organisms may have it in for Homo sapiens appeared on my computer screen last

104

week. I found a poem in the morning after leaving my computer on all night for a Microsoft update. I have never read such a succinct indictment of the human species in iambic tetrameter. While I am aware that humans are accelerating the destruction of the biosphere, this poem indicated that in some parts of the biosphere there is no sympathy for the human condition. Given the literary genius of the poetry, I was sure the message didn't come from Microsoft. I suspected my resident carpenter ant, Cindi Camponotus, had been in communication with the culprits.

Over the next several days of communication with my insect neighbor, she revealed that the simultaneous global outbreak of COVID-19 was no coincidence. There is a vast anti-Homo sapiens conspiracy in operation. It is the product of a multi-species collaboration among Formicidae (ant) families which began several years ago. While the release of the virus was a well-orchestrated operation, the timing of the pandemic reveals major political schisms in the anti-human conspiracy that just may have saved humans from extinction.

Quoting from Ms. Camponotus' notes, "Fire ants created the virus in multiple underground laboratories using various bats and pangolins from wet markets. Ants generally help diseases jump hosts, but this time we were targeting coronaviruses for their stealth and virulence. Ants have figured out how to use human omnivorous stupidity to test spillover pathogens. Once developed, other ant species carry the virus around the globe to their underground colonies. There they wait for the signal to break out of their colonies and run across screens, surfaces, food, keyboards, phones, and doorknobs, spreading the virus among humans."

I asked Cindi why a family of insects would attack the human species, and Ms. Camponotus offered the following explanation: "You ask why ants? Ants are leading a multi-species global cooperative effort to take back the earth. Ants are a eusocial species, like Homo sapiens, and are therefore better equipped than any other organism to mount a long-term, disciplined strategy. We live in every corner of the globe. There are over twenty quadrillion of us on this earth."

"Why now," I asked Cindi.

She replied, "You are killing us. And Homo sapiens is exterminating itself anyway. Our goal is to speed up the processes. We are giving humans a little push over the edge. The only question is how many insect families will you kill off before you exterminate yourselves. It is a race to the death." I asked Cindi why ants chose to use a virus, and Ms. Camponotus explained, "We chose a human-specific virus because it would leave the rest of the biosphere intact, if not thriving. We are not fans of slash and burn aggression, like the primates in question."

"Well," I remarked to Cindi, "how is this working out for you all?"

"We made a few mistakes," explained an exasperated ant. "The fire ants were looking for a virus with long latency between infection and symptoms. We achieved a one-week dormancy period. But we did not achieve our lethality objective. Our COVID-19 is thirty times more deadly than the flu but still only results in about a 3 percent death rate. we were aiming for an 80 to 90 percent rate like ebola. The plan was to wait until the US stock market hit 30,000. That was our launch signal. But political expediency got in the way of science. The coalition lost patience."

The laboratory for virus creation began to make sense, but I wondered about the timing and the supposedly sagacious fire ants missing their lethality target. Cindi explained, "The timing was a problem because we needed to get the pandemic started before real scientists replaced the idiots that are now running the US government. In order to bring on the full pandemic in the US before the election, we had to cut off lethality testing and start the pandemic at Dow Jones 28,000 in December. If we waited until after the US election, there is a good chance that the US would put scientists in charge of pandemics, and the scientists would shut down the pandemic before it became species-threatening. I fear that we may have rushed the project and used an inferior virus. I am not blaming the fire ants. The decision was a coalition consensus."

"Well, it appears that you have failed to extirpate Homo sapiens from its dominance. Are you done yet?" I asked.

An angry Cindi responded, "No way. There are secondary effects that will run their course over the next two years. There will be successive waves of this pandemic until humans succeed in developing a universal vaccine. That gives us about two years. These waves will be global and wear down economies to the point of human starvation and widespread violent food riots, especially in poor countries where people cannot wash their hands. The resulting migrations will cause wars. There is a good chance that global warming catastrophes will exacerbate the situation so that both disaster relief and medical systems are overwhelmed. Millions of deaths from this pandemic will be followed by many more millions from incompetent human responses to other natural events. Wars will add to the death toll—you can expect an increasing number. New pathogens will evolve. We have started something huge. As we say, 'The opera isn't over until the fire ants sing.'"

The Formicidae family has not given up hope. Cindi's parting remark was, "Consider this an early trial. We are playing the long game. Our strength is the leadership of superorganisms that have evolved over 168 million years. Formicidae philosophies that favored the ego over the community died with their champions. Your weakness is that you live to consume. When denied, you explode in fits of self-pity, revenge, corruption, and villainy. Many of you, who have fortified your nests with firearms and ammunition, will perish from fights over scarce resources. Even if we fail with the coronavirus, the fire ant lab technicians continue to work in wet markets wherever humans chew up and swallow natural ecosystems. There will be other, more lethal pandemics.

We have survived 168 million years as the largest eusocial superorganism on earth. We can wait a few more years for the end of the Anthropocene."

I thanked her for her candid if not ominous remarks. It is sobering to note that ants are capable of reaching across species boundaries to unite in the war against their common enemy, Homo sapiens. We don't usually associate such sagacity with hexapods. It appears that the politics of expediency compromised their current pandemic plan. Was it their haste to achieve their political objective that saved humanity? Maybe the next time, Homo Sapiens won't be so lucky.

Anthony Picardi

Then again, if humans could cooperate as effectively as ants, maybe Homo sapiens could avoid its own extinction by a diminutive creature with six hands.

Your Introduction to the Queen

october 2019

the queen asked me about you the other day. that kind of thing usually doesn't end well. i tried to put a positive spin on your bona fides. this is my statement.

'he is a seventy-one-year-old male homo sapiens in the last years of life. he has replaced running with amber ale. he no longer dives off zodiacs headfirst in scuba gear like lloyd bridges.

early on his mother told him stories of bullies in harbor springs. she told him never to be a weak marshmallow. that inspired the following:

in third grade, while still in the larval stage, he smashed a classmate, who was cutting in line, over the head with his lunch pail.

later he walked away from a scout ritual in protest. he got banished to the woods.

then he incited a pledge rebellion at his fraternity. he got denied all temporal happiness.

then he told venture capitalists that the president of his company committed fraud with a sharpie. he got fired.

then he accused the county planning commission of misfeasance. he got terminated.

now he is after the fascists who are taking over the country. i wonder how this will end.

his mother also told him about her experience with predatory priests. this may have soured him on religion. to my knowledge, he has not yet attacked a priest. i think he is proud of his uncompromising crusade against bullies and injustice. at times, though, it gets annoying. he may be editing my reports.

to his credit, he has not been indicted by the wee-too sisters. he is flying under their radar by doing the cooking.

also to his credit, he is one of the few homo sapiens who really gets the moral imperatives of living in a eusocial community, like ours. he learned about us from reading e. o. wilson's ant research. he knows that eusocial communities may not be unique in the milky way, but he also knows that no one out there cares if homo sapiens goes extinct.

your highness, dr. lepidoptera, as we call him, is an increasingly decrepit specimen who has been mentally and physically scarred since his larval stage. he rebels against authority. he has trouble walking. he could never survive in an ant colony.

but he needs to be commended since he will eventually leave his estate to us rather than another horrible herd of homo sapiens offspring that will slink around and poison us. dr. lepidoptera is on our side. he is harmless.'

that is what i testified, boss. she did not ask me to serve you with a subpoena. you are okay for a while. stay out of trouble.

factually reported and respectfully submitted as per agreement by cindi camponotus, official holly point farm investigative reporter

Ode to the Model Railroad

october 2019

past cindis have called you boss, so i will continue the trope. the sobriquet implies a modicum of respect but in no way entitles you to tell me how to live or boss me around. i toured your railroad layout. it is scaled for carpenter ants. nice job. we may move in. it reflects a certain attitude. Here are my thoughts.

in bronze you stand on granite stone,
the creator of this town you own.
upon the tower of brick edifice
perches a giant leucocephalus.

light through its fenestrations
shows, a non-religious celebration;
fish and birds and ho chi minh,
and the galaxy we all live in.

what does this village symbolize,
smaller than lilliputian size.
when you squint your eyes,
you see names of friends you recognize.

Grain train rumbles through the town of Picardi

no tarted paint hiding
naked weathered siding.
this is a place you cannot find;
the creation of a fertile mind.
from afar the scene looks real.
it has a worn and dusty feel.

did all these people who you know
really do the things you show.
maybe not, maybe so.
it doesn't matter, this is art.
in the scenes they do their part.

is honest john selling weed.
does an alligator really feed
on grazing longhorn steers.
do gherkins and spears chase away fears.

vreeland is brewing beers.
karen is kanning pulchritude,
while kent is serving asian food.
sherry's selling mystery books,
while carolyn is training cooks.

City of Pulchritude industries

a fire flickers in the woods.
an ivory-billed glides between the trees,
above a bald cypress swamp of tea.

seagulls squabble, laugh and squawk,
diving for fish dropped from the dock
of vaskys and freed's cannery,
while a great-white glides by silently.

steam pulsates, wheels squeal, pistons pound,
the orange-and-red daylight rounds the curve into town.

two long, two short, one double long whistle sounds,
clackety-clacking through the crossing,
screeching to a halt, heavy breathing, panting steam,
waiting for passengers to step down.

the staccato bell ding, ding, dings as the luxury ride
groans forward, and creeps out of town.

no scandals or criminality,
no litter or depravity.
like a well-run ant colony,
all is ordered and tranquility;
impossible for a human city.

creator and ruler of sixty square feet,
you decide
what to build and who abides.
after toiling like a god,
you rested,
satisfied.

boss, your art is nice, but we would not complement the
scenery. we prefer a more subterranean abode. somewhere
we will not be run over by a train.

factually reported and respectfully submitted as per agreement by cindi camponotus, official holly point farm investigative reporter

Letter to the MIT
Class of 1970

Editor's Note: The "Letter to the MIT Class of 1970" was first published in the MIT Class of 1970 50th reunion book, May 2020. This letter includes Cindi's testimony as the only non-Homo sapiens to comment on the state of the environment on Earth Day 2020.

Earth Day 2020

Dear Classmates:

I volunteered to write a report on the environment for our class on this 50th anniversary of Earth Day. We can all agree that humanity's impact on the environment is enormous. In my opinion, the largest share of environmental problems can be traced to global warming and natural habitat loss. At the global level this environmental crisis is causing a species extinction rate conservatively estimated to be 1,000 times faster than the last global extinction that wiped out the dinosaurs along with 76 percent of life on the planet.

For a detailed scientific account of global warming, I strongly recommend you explore the International Panel on Climate

Change (IPCC) web site. I will not go into details here except to say that global warming is accelerating. The Paris Accord temperature limit of 1.5°C above pre-industrial levels will be exceeded since there are at present not enough serious country programs to stop greenhouse gas emissions fast enough.

Habitat loss is caused by the increase of our environmental footprint. Our environmental footprint is defined as the renewable resources humans use. These include: fishing grounds, built infrastructure, cropland, grazing land, forest land, and carbon adsorption capacity. Carbon adsorption capacity is the amount of unharvested forested land and ocean that is necessary to sequester emitted carbon. Only these five renewable resources are considered as they are necessary for all people globally to sustain life. While nonrenewable resources like coal, copper, or lithium may be useful for a certain quality of life, they are not essential, and the mining of them uses nonrenewable resources. According to the Global Footprint Network, which has calculated the footprints for all countries in the world, humanity today uses the equivalent of 1.8 Earths to provide the renewable resources needed to feed ourselves, support our infrastructure, and absorb our waste. We are degrading our renewable resources.

I find it encouraging that young people are starting to find their voices. Some are angry that the "adults," in particular our political leaders, cannot find the moral courage to do anything about global warming. Fifteen-year-old Greta Thunberg exemplified this outrage at the UN climate talks on September 23, 2019.

When considering environmental issues, it is instructive to hear from the non-human life forms that are affected by human activities. They have no voice in our political systems. Yet many must depend on Homo sapiens to save them from extinction. Powerless relative to Homo sapiens, it is hard to blame them if they get angry along with our teenagers. The class of '70 spoke truth to power. In that spirit, I have asked a resident of my farm to share her views on environmental issues with us. What follows is the transcript of our conversation, which took place over numerous nights when she laboriously entered her answers on my computer keyboard, letter by letter.

TP—Please state your name and occupation.

CC—My name is Cindi Camponotus, Formicidae family, carpenter ant, and investigative reporter, currently residing in the fallen sweetgum in the woods on Holly Point Farm.

TP—What expertise do you bring to this inquiry?

CC—I am connected to a global ecosystem of insects, traveling birds, plants, and the mycorrhizal layer of fungi. I am conversant with Homo sapiens' messages via SSL packets leaked from cuts we make in fiber optic cables. We in the Formicidae family are a successful eusocial species whose genome has evolved over 168 million years. We survived the Cretaceous extinction.

TP—For the record of ant-skeptics, how do you communicate with other species?

CC—For you, I push down computer keys one at a time. For other species, we have methods which you have yet to figure out.

TP—So what can you tell us about the state of the environment?

CC—You are killing us. The population of insects has declined in Europe and the Americas to a fourth or an eighth of what it was thirty years ago. Forty percent of insect species are in decline. At that rate there will be none of us left by the end of the century.

TP—Well, we will not miss fruit flies and mosquitoes. Are my lepidopteran friends at risk?

CC—Pollinators are declining, and you know that your beehives collapsed last year. Songbirds migrating from the tropics say in some forests ground insects have declined by 90 percent. Wild bird populations in the continental U.S. and Canada have declined by 30 percent since 1970, with a 53 percent decline in grassland birds and a 37 percent decline in shorebirds. Insect-eating tropical birds have declined by 50 percent. To answer your question, how many butterflies did you see in southern France last spring?

TP—Only a few.

CC—Insects have a narrow thermal reproductive band. Tropical forest high temperatures have increased 4°F, too hot for many. We insects are at the bottom of the food chain. Thirty-five percent of your crops are pollinated by insects. Your food supply is at risk.

TP—You seem biased toward your insect buddies. As a lepidopterist, I sympathize.

CC—There is more. Coral reefs are bleaching and dying off

because of ocean warming. Oceanic diatoms, which sequester carbon when they die and end up in ocean sediments, are declining due to ocean acidification. This is one factor causing global warming to accelerate. There is a gyre of litter twice the size of Texas in the Pacific off California. Laughing gulls tell me it is killing oceanic birds, sea mammals, turtles, and fish. Plastics and chemicals are concentrating in the food chain. Migrators tell me the Amazon forest, their winter home, is burning. As I write this, Australia is burning. This affects humans' ability to fight new pandemics brought on by global warming since the rain forest is where many of your life-saving drugs originate.

TP—So is it about loss of habitat and biodiversity?

CC—There are serious physical effects of global warming. Sea level rise is accelerating and could increase by several meters in the lifetime of your children if aggressive measures are not taken to stop global warming. Wildfires are larger and occur more often. Tropical storms are more frequent and violent. River flooding is more common and lethal heat waves more frequent and severe. Shall I continue?

TP—Okay, how many of these can we do something about?

CC—All these are caused by you, Homo sapiens, so you tell me.

TP—Well, you are a smart ant. What do you recommend we do?

CC—You humans are taking over natural habitats everywhere. You are destroying whole ecosystems. Most habitats have keystone species. When they are eliminated from the environment, like corals from shallow seas, native grasses from savannahs, upper-story trees from rain forests, or apex predators, entire complex networks of interdependent species in the habitat vanish. I think there are too many Homo sapiens.

TP—Human population growth is slowing because of the demographic transition. There are fewer people living in poverty. When people are better off, population growth slows and even reverses, to the extent that women get educated and enter the market economy.

CC—Yes, but the acquisition of manufactured stuff continues to increase. There is no indication that the per capita human ecological footprint will stop growing. Your MIT research on dematerialization concludes that technological inventions will not stop overuse of resources.

TP—Technology has always enabled humans to produce enough to fulfill our wants and needs, despite dire predictions in the past.

CC—In 1970, the ecological footprint of the global population was about equal to the capacity of the globe to sustain the human population with renewable resources. Since then humanity's footprint has doubled. In the USA, the per capita footprint is three times the global average. Even if human population growth slows to zero, consumption per person will still grow. Regardless of technology, the more you produce, the more renewable resources you will use for the endless amount of stuff you consume.

TP—Hey, humans can use technology to live cleaner with a lighter footprint. For example, the farm we live on is conservation land, which will never be developed. I drive a hybrid car, recycle trash, compost biologicals, and refuse to fly on airplanes. I can supply my own food from a vegetable garden, hunt deer and harvest fish, oysters and crabs from the creek.

CC—Thanks for the farm. It was ours anyway. But you are kidding about the garden...really? First, you are too lazy to raise all your own food. Second, you and Shirley live on sixty-four acres here. It would take five USAs for everyone to live at your population density. And a lot of you would be living in the Grand Canyon. The problem with you rural folks is that you look around and think you are still living in the wilderness. The birds tell me horror stories about your big cities with no trees, legions of cats and cellphone towers. However you figure it, there are too many people.

TP—Okay, I get it. We live high off the hog here and in the USA generally. Engineers will find a solution. This is MIT you are talking to. Show a little optimism. Technology has brought us the green revolution, potable water, elimination of more and more diseases, safe housing, transportation systems that the Romans would envy, food made from oil, artificial skin, and Wikipedia. At MIT there are a host of research projects on how to deal with global warming; like liquid metal grid batteries, energy-efficient building design, molten salt nuclear reactors, air-breathing batteries, high-efficiency solar cells, low-cost solar for off-grid communities and community solar cooperatives, flexible semi-conducting films, grid-connected wind farms, and low-energy nuclear reactions, to name a few.

CC—It is not enough. Current research will take years or even decades to make a significant impact. By comparison, the proliferation of iPhones was easy.

TP—So what kinds of solutions do we need, if not these new technologies?

CC—Implementing new technologies, infrastructure, and management systems on a global scale is much harder. Humans will have to change economic and social norms and values—what it means to be human. And you only have about a decade to do this before the climate goes into positive feedback warming mode and becomes impossible to reverse. If everyone is going to continue to be better off, your species will have to learn to control its population growth as well as its per capita consumption. Or many more species will be extirpated.

TP—How do you know about large-scale change?

CC—I have 300,000 sisters in our rotten log. We live in a consensus community. It is hard work convincing the sisters to harvest a grasshopper corpse. And the negotiation that goes into moving the colony is intense. That takes cooperation and discipline. It took us millions of years to learn how to work together. And you need to do this on a global scale in a decade.

TP—Well, you ants have rather strict rules. Humans are a lot more creative.

CC—We have leadership. Homo sapiens does not. In an ant colony, if folks pursue their own ends at the expense of the colony, that is treason.

TP—We got together and passed the Paris Climate Accord.

CC—Passing it was easy. Implementing it takes leadership. Your commitment was fragile. I hear you are dropping out of it. You are missing the deadline to stop the rise of global temperatures to 1.5°C. Now you must do some massive carbon sequestration and use massive energy storage and nuclear base load power. You will have to seriously change your lifestyle, change the prices for everything containing carbon, recycle manufactured stuff, and eliminate biological waste, just for starters.

TP—We could do that.

CC—But you won't.

TP—You take a dim view of Homo sapiens. Why won't we solve global warming?

CC—To be clear, you could solve it. But you won't because you are genetically deficient.

TP—Sounds a bit racist coming from an ant.

CC—You do not have a stewardship gene. We are both eusocial animals. We are both products of individual and group natural selection. These forces oppose each other. Individual selection promotes an individual's genes while group selection promotes the genes that enable altruism and cooperation.

TP—So Homo sapiens is genetically inferior to ants?

CC—After a hundred million years of evolution, we ants became expert at group selection by competing with other colonies. But we never got so populous that we threatened all other species.

TP—So humans have once again gone where no species has gone before.

CC—For humans, stewardship is an intellectual concept. It is not genetically based. It is an enormous effort for you to promote stewardship against the selfish forces of individual natural selection.

TP—It is true we have had some spectacular failures. We have only been around for 200,000 years as Homo sapiens. Now we have global institutions. We are making progress.

CC—You don't have time. Your evolution to a global eusocial community has to succeed in the next generation at the same time that huge investments are made by leaders in global warming mitigation and habitat preservation and restoration. We insects feel your failure. We don't believe you will make it.

TP—So you are giving up on Homo sapiens.

CC—You look like a failed species. I have written a poem for your epitaph.

TP—Isn't this a bit premature?

CC—Possibly. If enough of you read your own epitaph and think about it with your big heads, maybe you will find a way to keep from harming the rest of us. In the end, enough of us will survive to start over. Ants will still be here.

TP—Okay. Thank you, Ms. Cindi, for your remarks and your endurance in pushing down the keys. I appreciate your perspective. With our big heads, we get arrogant at times. We are newcomers. I will post the poem you wrote.

End of transcript.

Classmates, the following poem is written by Cindi Camponotus to shake humanity out of its environmental lethargy before it is too late. You may find it depressing and inappropriate for a 50th reunion party. However, I suggest you consider it in the same genre as the writings of Rachel Carson, Garrett Hardin, MIT's Jay Forrester, and Dennis and Donella Meadows. Many others have described the consequences of exponential human growth. Is it too much to imagine that non-humans in the biosphere may have a message for us? This is from a carpenter ant. It is short. And she cannot capitalize.

Kind regards,

Tony Picardi

the short run species
by
cindi camponotus

homo sapiens had a short run.
compared to others, its reign just begun.
you should have survived at least as long
as the primate group to which you belong.

over billions of years, life from the past
was sequestered in carbon, which you burned too fast.
in three hundred years you caused so much heat
that from runaway swelter, there was no retreat.

your intelligence was your unique specialty,
but you failed to adapt to earth's reality.
in the rocks below, your plastics persist.
by all other creatures you won't be missed.

with no people around, there'll be no history,
so, the passing of humans won't be a mystery.
no one will know you were ever there.
surviving life forms will not even care.

respectfully submitted by cindi camponotus, official holly
point farm investigative reporter

The Parable of
the Red Hat

september 2020

she absconded with all your red hats.

Who?

your wife.

Why?

because she doesn't want to be seen with a person wearing a symbol.

They were my sailing hats. They had the class logo embroidered.

she said, from far away, you looked like a red-hatted fascist.

Oh my! My friends all know I am not a right-wing, supremacist, fascist idiot.

it's the folks you don't know who will think you may hate them. she wants to get along with everyone.

I want my red hats back.

she will give them back when he is gone.

When will that be?

months, a year, never... how can i tell

Why is my red hat so dangerous?

it could get you into serious trouble. where i come from, we use scent pheromones. we have to recognize each other in the dark. someone comes into the colony wearing the wrong cologne, as you say, they get dragged out by the guards, de-limbed and thrown on the compost heap.

Isn't that a little harsh?

we don't want the fugitives to run away on us, do we.

I am glad we don't have pheromones.

you have facebook.

What has that got to do with hats?

it feeds you concentrated soup of your own regurgitated juices. these are seasoned with messages that are paid for by whoever wants to take over your brain. i know this because we regurgitate to each other on scouting runs. a little garlic goes a long way.

Well, Facebook is just free speech.

when this happens to us, it is because a predatory genus has attacked our colony and is about to make us slaves.

How does that work?

the message starts as a low-concentration alarm pheromone; then they turn up the concentration until the whole colony panics. ants run around confused, not knowing who is friend or foe. colony defenders don't know what to do. meanwhile, the enemy carries off the eggs and larvae and makes them slaves.

Where did she put my hats?

they are hidden until he leaves.

These hats are my identity.

they are a symbol. you humans are all about symbols.

It is not about what is ON my head; it is about what is IN my head.

but what is on your head is a symbol of what is in your head.

Is there any way I can symbolize I am not a fascist?

of course, it is obvious.

How?

wear a white hat.

factually reported and respectfully submitted as per agreement by cindi camponotus, official holly point farm investigative reporter

The Trial

Editor's Note: "The Trial" was first published in *The Dead Mule School of Southern Literature*, August 2021.

september 2020

boss, it happened again. more russian spies. white house roaches were tried today. i was drafted to be the judge. my elevation to the bench was because the prosecutors figured i was unbiased on account of a carpenter ant can't eat a death's head cockroach without the help of fifty sisters. my judicial credentials are a matter of public record after i successfully prosecuted the illicit honeydew traders and their treasonous conspiracy with a carnivorous caterpillar. i insisted the trial be fair, like in an ant colony, with witnesses and evidence.

the fbi—the feral bird investigators—found a score of roaches in the woods traveling south. our birds-in-blue had them corralled on the ground. the prosecution consisted of a flock of blue jays locally known as 'the jeering jays.'

although the evidence was clear—undocumented roaches were caught sneaking through the underbrush, diplomatic complications emerged. i could tell by their ushanka hats they were russians. the suspects in question, a species called blaberus craniifer, aka the death's head cockroach, are locust-sized, stink like a garbage-pile tramp, and are as greasy as a punk's spiky hairdo. this was going to be dicey and dangerous. events proved me right.

The Russian suspects were death's head cockroaches

the prosecution periodically pecked at the defendants to keep them cowering in a stinking scrum. 'jeer jeer jeer, down on yer bellies, ya stinking roaches, jeer jeer.'

the jury assembled in the tree tops. it was a murder of fifty-three crows. 'caw caw caw caw, off with their heads, tear 'em apart, off with their heads.'

i had to shout magisterial commands to be heard. 'the prisoners will stand, raise their two front tarsi, state their names, and swear to tell the truth, the whole truth, under pain of sextuple tarsal severance.'

the cowed roaches responded one by one—'aras, boris, igor, vlad, lev, jared, felix, mikhail, oleg, vitaly, bannonika, dmitry, natalia, konstantin, viktor, ivanka, semion, sergei, vladimir, gennady... your honor.'

the crows dropped down a few branches. 'caw caw, off with their heads.'

i yelled, 'the jury will remain quiet. the prosecution will present its case.'

the prosecutor jay landed on a rock facing the huddle of roaches. he raised his blue topknot and trained his white-rimmed black eye on the suspects. 'the charges are 'traveling while alien.' we will show that these roaches intend to take over our habitat and ruin our way of life. they plan to perpetrate pernicious crimes. they will upset ecological equilibrium. they will spread deadly, disgusting disease and germs. we ask the jury to consider whether they are safe to eat or will ingestion of them in the community lead to gastrointestinal distress, psychotic hallucinations, or even heart disease. we ask for the maximum penalty of death by mastication.'

some of the jury moved down closer. 'caw caw caw, off with their heads. caw caw, gobble them up, caw caw caw caw.'

i had to shout again. 'the jury will remain silent or be held in contempt of court.' to the defendants i asked, 'what is your defense. what is a band of super-sized apparatchik death's head roaches doing in our woods.'

the defense was led by a katydid, ms. pseudotettigony acrimonious, known for leading the 'katydid acrimonies' in partisan chants at pep rallies.

a lime-green ms. acrimonious tiptoed out from behind a sweet-gum leaf and hung swaying over the defendants. 'roaches are diplomats from white house. roaches from mother russia here to get kompromat on moose and squirrel. roaches have diplomat immunity, have passports from vladimir, personal-like. you hear truth from rudy boltonnovitch.'

the prosecution interrupted. 'objection. jeer jeer jeer jeer. no witnesses. no spies telling lies.'

135

"We ask for the maximum penalty of death by mastication."

the jury erupted again. 'caw caw caw caw, spies spies, caw, spies.'

i shouted. 'overruled. trials have witnesses. the jury will remain quiet. the witness will testify.'

rudy boltonnovitch, his face covered with white hairs and his thorax boasting a black skull looking like the work of a tattoo artist on lsd, stretched up on four feet and waved his front tarsi back and forth in a sign of surrender.

'we look a little funny but we don't tell any lies.
we are honest diplomats who never work as spies.
all the crimes you hear about us are done by other guys.'

the jury got agitated. they hopped from branch to branch over the defendants, some moving closer. they pecked at leaves and bark, which fell down on the defendants, 'caw caw caw, no witnesses, eat them eat them, caw caw caw.'

the prosecution jay cocked his head and considered the murder of crows. 'the prosecution will admit no witness testimony. these roaches are lying spies.' with that, the big blue jay hopped down from his rock and impaled rudy boltonnovich with his stiletto beak, thrashed him against the rock until he broke into several pieces, and then gulped down rudy's parts. the jay wiped drops of saturated fat off his beak and called, 'jeer jeer jeer jeer.'

concerned that i was losing control of my trial, i responded, 'i remind the prosecution to maintain a civil demeanor in these proceedings. we will hear from witnesses and they will not be eaten unless convicted. ms. acrimonious, call your next witness.'

council for the defense, with only her green eyes peeking over her sweetgum leaf, 'mister lev will tell story of white house.'

seeing his comrade succumb to whatever laws of nature operated for the prosecution, lev sang like a sparrow at a seed-fest. 'glorious rasputin spy caper is blow up—white house too dangerous. full of rats. is battle of rats. backbiting, treachery, murder, poisoning. moose like raging bull. rats purged for being 'enemy of people'. sending messages leaving bloody roach prints on computer. we send for help to volodya—president putin to you. he says abandon mission. shred and flush 'useful idiots' list. flush evidence of rasputin caper and enemies list down toilet. flush three times. get out of town. run for merry lago. hide in palm trees. become tree roaches and listen for kompromat. we make tracks south for merry lago.'

once again, the jury erupted. 'caw caw caw, eat them, eat them, caw caw.'

'silence,' i yelled.

in a desperate attempt to turn even one juror in favor of the friendless roaches, ms. acrimonious delivered a poetic plea.

'we are honest little bugs who do not consort with thugs.

we are having many scruples while we launder all our rubles.

there is nothing that's illegal from our alternating facts

which we spin into conspiracies and send to you with pacs.'

all of the prosecution jays screeched, 'jeer jeer jeer, no witnesses. guilty guilty. eat them, eat the green female liars. eat the green liars.'

i shouted, 'order order order orrrrrrrrrrrrrrrrrrrrrdeeeerrrr.'

ignoring my pleas, the prosecutor jay jumped up and snatched ms. acrimonious, beating her on a rock before swallowing her headfirst, whole. several other jays snatched up the rest of the green defense team before they could spread their wings. i considered what to do since it appeared that the case for the defense was literally devoured.

seeing the demise of their roach comrade, the collapse of their case, and the court's inability to enforce rule of law, the roaches lost all faith in the criminal justice system. they broke out of their huddle. they charged a jay en masse, who jumped up, opening an escape route. roaches rushed out in panic, scrambling over each other to get out from under the jury and into the shadows. the jury erupted in a cacophony of caws. 'caw caw caw caw, eat them, eat them, grab the stinking bugs, caw caw, eat them, all lousy spies, don't let them escape. chew before you swallow. caw caw caw.' a flapping mass of black crows descended upon the fleeing crowd of death's head roaches like a tornado in a black squall. wings batted branches as a waterfall of jurists descended, screaming, 'caw caw.' beaks thrusted, snap and clack. roaches were flipped up, snatched, and cut in two. the murder of crows herded the pitiful band of comrades into the open, jabbing with the pent-up energy of frustration, hunger, and wicked table manners. soon the kerfuffle abated. black feathers floated down. fifty-three crows crowded on the ground, pecking at

Judicial proceedings turned feeding frenzy

the remains of former diplomats, 'caw cawing' among themselves. 'how did the one with the long red scarf taste. these are greasy little buggers. hey, can i get more than just legs over here, caw caw caw.'

none of the suspects made it to merry lago. as i write this, i imagine the basement of the white house full of bloated dead rats and bloody roach prints on the computer server. i imagine a bull moose kicking over lamps and breaking china in a stalinesque rage about 'enemies of the people.'

boss, we got rid of aliens. but my judicial proceeding turned into a feeding frenzy. i should have expected that given the tenuous status of the rule of law these days. once a murder of crows assembles for a jury, there is little hope that reason will prevail.

factually reported and respectfully submitted as per agreement by cindi camponotus, official holly point farm investigative reporter and amateur magistrate

Human Tastes

Editor's Note:

We feasted on a Boston butt which lasted for four person-meals. This morning it was time to pull pork, resulting in another four person-meals. While pulling our butt, I mused upon the flavor of succulent roasted pork. I have read anthropological studies of "uncivilized" tribes in the South Pacific who describe the taste of human flesh as comparable to that of a well-roasted pig. I do not know of any account of specific preparations, spices, or marinades used for such dishes. It seems probable that all preparations of humans would have been "naked." While packaging lumps of roasted butt, I decided to find out what human beings taste like.

Clearly, I could not personally carve up and roast people. Such culinary experiments would seem unneighborly and may even violate Virginia statutes. Preferring to remain within the law, I outsourced the research. I naturally turned to my chief investigator of all things natural hereabouts, Cindi Camponotus. I charged her with scientifically determining the major flavors of Homo sapiens and reporting back. I rewarded her team of carpenter ant comrades, in advance, with two fresh house sparrows (alien in our state) tenderized by a twenty-gauge.

Afterward, I congratulated Cindi for her accomplishment. No human could have done as well on account of government

142

regulations. And certainly, no human institution could have produced such a comprehensive report within the budget of a few dead house sparrows.

april 2021

boss, different people have different tastes. i never would have figured that until you commissioned me to investigate the matter of human flavors. of course, i couldn't do this personally, just as you cannot, but for different reasons. while carpenter ants of genus camponotus are omnivores, sometimes relishing fresh meat, we are loath to take on a homo sapiens, being vastly outweighed. our comrades the fire ants, however, attempt to kill humans as a regular sport with the result that they have brought the whole arsenal of human biochemical warfare down upon themselves. we limit our ambitions in this regard. we jump on struggling locusts or cart away and dismember out-of-tune cicadas. certain of our tribe show up at summer picnics hosted by dead racoons and squirrels. but dead humans have been too scarce since the plagues of the 1300s for us to evolve a homo sapiens gastronomy. the present pandemic, if successful, may leave the landscape littered with enough dead humans for us to evolve a culture for ingesting your neighbors. but for now, i needed a small swarm from the culicidae family.

mosquitoes around your farm have been nearly extirpated on account of your anti-rain-gutter philosophy and the vicious schools of gambusia minnows you keep in your fishpond. they gulp down mosquito larvae like a german shepherd on a bratwurst. since your common tiger mosquito is a homebody, never venturing more than several shade trees from a puddle, i had to conduct this research in the nearest cosmopolitan center, onancock. thanks for the ride, boss.

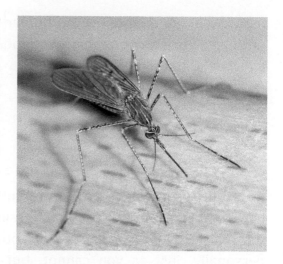

i used a latin square statistical design with age, sex, and political persuasion treatments. this required a minimum sample of 270 bites to show significant differences using chi-square statistics. onancock has a bounty of rain gutters, a willing host of humans to parasitize, and a plethora of unscreened porches. given the abundance of 'volunteers,' i upped my game and opted for a multiple regression analysis requiring a sample of 900 bites. allowing for a non-trivial number of my field-workers to be swatted and their samples splatted, i therefore recruited a force of 3,000 tiger mosquitoes in lovely onancock.

data were recorded by nine geometer moth caterpillars, known to the entomologically illiterate as 'measuring worms.' crosstabulations yielded these results:

1. men have base palates of stale perspiration with hints of gunpowder, burnt hydrocarbons, and dead fish.

2. women are bifurcated, with some having base palates of earth, weeds, and mixed herbs, while the rest have a base palate of various detergents.

3. most humans under the age of eighteen have no discernable taste. those who do have a hint of scented tobacco and marijuana.

political persuasion was measured by proxy. those bitten while watching the fox channel were labeled 'republican,' while those bitten while watching msnbc were labeled 'democrat.' the results of this associative analysis revealed top notes to the human meal. republicans have sour notes with a bitter aftertaste. democrats tend toward the sweet end of the palate with a large diversity of top notes—some reminiscent of loblolly pine and some hinting of passion fruit. this is evidence for the hypothesis that people are what they taste like.

a word of caution. this experiment produced correlations but did not show causality. if republicans act vengeful and xenophobic, is the reason because these actions have permeated their flesh and caused them to taste sour and bitter. or are republicans sour and bitter to their core, and that is what predicts their behavior. likewise, does the sweetness and diversity of a democrat's top note explain his/her habit of falling victim to despots and liars. or have democrats always been wimps to their cores with a lack of bile and stomach acid, resulting in sweet chops.

i note that these results may be influenced by geography. for example, if i did this experiment in the midwest, would all humans taste like marbled beef.

factually reported and respectfully submitted as per agreement by cindi camponotus, official holly point farm investigative reporter

The results revealed top notes to the human meal

25

Epitaph for Bugs Bunny

Editor's Note: "Epitaph for Bugs Bunny" was first published in *The Dead Mule School of Southern Literature*, July 2021.

july, 2021

we found the remains of a large rabbit in your garden a few months ago. alas, poor bugs, i knew him, boss. a rabbit of infinite energy and most excellent taste. from his bleached skull hung lips that have tasted uncountable blooms. here was encased a sensuous nose that twitched at mellifluous scents and odious chemicals alike. here lived a brain that spawned neither malice nor prevarication. bugs, where be your gambols now, your flashes of cottontail, your piles of pellets.

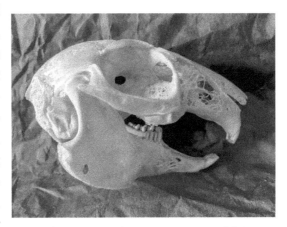

Alas, poor bugs was a rabbit of infinite energy and most excellent taste.

Bugs was a civilized hare

bugs died in your flower meadow. many others have died in field and meadow, unsung—their remains scattered, reclaimed by scavengers and fungi. but bugs' ears were tickless. he was a civilized hare. when his term was over, he surrendered gracefully. he nestled down among his favorite flowers and viewed his last dream. his nostrils flared and his haunches twitched while he dreamt—bounding down a grassy path to his favorite patch of monarda. he severed a stalk of bee balm. it disappeared between his grinding molars, leaf by leaf then tasty bloom. he had table manners.

boss, we ants have done our duty with mr. bunny's softer parts. his skeleton remains. now it is time you carved some stone and sent a message. lay down granite tonnage. make it clear that animals that don't bite are honored members of this farm— they are 'non-ticks.' use bugs as an example. reconstruct his fractured skull and build a memorial. what do we say about this mild-mannered rodent. be generous to bugs. be expansive. this will become history. i suggest the following epitaph:

'here we honor all who fell in defense of rabbit rights. we honor those who wore the gray and the cottontail and fell in defense of personal government. they struggled for self-determination. they died true to the principles upon which all true rabbits live. they knew their rights and dared to maintain them. reproduction was their sacred duty. they were prodigious populators. they bravely died in the talons of rapacious raptors. many fell to the hunter's gun, ending up in pots. none braver bled for a cause so grand as their sacred genome.'

now, boss, what message do we send about carnivorous flies.

respectfully submitted as per agreement by cindi camponotus, official holly point farm investigative reporter

Infection

Editor's Note: "Infection" was published in *The Dead Mule School of Southern Literature*, January 2023.

november 2021

boss, our colony was destroyed. many of us were turned into zombie ants. it started one morning a week ago. i noticed a forager hanging over the colony. she was locked immobile onto a branch by her mandibles. i figured she was resting in the namaste ant pose—relaxing before a long and tedious pill-bug shift. the yoga-before-pill-bug practice helps your foraging sister focus. it puts her in touch with her inner ant. she was still there in the afternoon, but now her eyes were milky white, her legs were sticking straight out, and there was a mushroom sprouting from her neck. i looked around. there were other foragers climbing slowly up into the same shrub overhanging the colony. i saw another hanging from her mandibles. yikes, i thought. i needed to alert antoinette fauchietta, our colony disease doctor.

i hustled to her underground lab. waving my antennae wildly, i jabbered, 'doctor fauchietta, ants are hanging from branches by their mandibles. i saw one with a mushroom cap sprouting from her neck.'

Ant attacked by fungus

doctor fauchietta responded in the calm, measured tone of a scientist. 'my little sister, this is the malignant ophiocordyceps fungal disease known to infest carpenter ant colonies. in the medical profession, we call the disease ophio-19.'

'where does it come from,' i asked.

'we live in rotten logs on the forest floor, in and around the fungus mycorrhizal layer. when an ant picks up a fungal spore, the fungus grows inside the sister. it eventually sprouts its fruiting body, a mushroom cap. this cap contains thousands of spores that rain down on the forest floor which in turn infect other ants and other insects who walk underneath.'

Anthony Picardi

'is there a cure. what can we do to stop this.'

'lamentably, there is no cure,' doctor fauchietta replied. 'the fungus releases psilocybin—a psychedelic drug that takes over our nervous system and turns ants into zombies. it commands the victim to seek an elevated place and lock on to a branch in a death grip. you can tell the infected ones. they walk around stiff-legged, looking for bushes to do their 'skylarking', as we call it.'

i was becoming desperate. 'are we all going to die.'

doctor fauchietta eyed me with her five thousand lenses. 'not if you take strict precautions immediately. first you must wash all spores off your body. i don't mean an ant bath where you lick yourself. if you do this, you will ingest spores and become infected. find a puddle and splash in the water. next round up the healthy workers and escape from the rain of these deadly spores. go into quarantine.'

the good doctor paused. she tilted her head, and her antennae pointed straight at me. 'now comes the hard part. pay attention now. be strong. leave behind any workers that appear to be zombies. prevent them from escaping with you by any means. if you have to, kill them before they infect you. when you get to your quarantine site, evict all infected ants. this will be hard. but if you don't follow these rules, everyone in our colony will die.'

i paused to absorb this news. 'okay, i get it. this is science. i am glad you will be with us to enforce the rules.'

doctor fauchietta replied, 'i will try. i have been giving zombie ants steroid drug cocktails. none have worked. once a zombie, always a zombie. i will see you at the quarantine site.' tired, she ambled slowly away.

i needed help. i called a meeting of the wee-too sisters. nan pelosis arrived first. her ancestors founded the wee-too female ant solidarity movement 140 million years ago. this is the reason why all eusocial ant colonies are run by females. their master stroke came 120 million years ago when they crafted the solution to male domination. the highest court in those days was packed with drunken sex deviants who called themselves the craven-gnaws, after their habit of noshing fermented hackberries. the craven-gnaws were about to legalize a dangerous sexual behavior known as the dragonfly flutter. this often resulted in broken necks for the female participant.

in bold, direct action, nan pelosis' ancestors organized a cadre of wee-toos to arrest the drunken craven-gnaw judges. they were 'impeached' on the thorns of a greenbriar vine winding up a peach tree. while the legality of the action was questionable, the colony, which was 98 percent female, believed justice was served.

'nan, we need to do something. doctor fauchietta says we need to separate the healthy ants from the zombies and escape to a quarantine site immediately.'

'relax,' said nan, 'i will get homeland security to arrest the zombies while we rescue the eggs.' we hustled off to the homeland security chamber. we explained the situation to general michelle flynflam and her deputy, rogita stones.

'fake news,' shouted general flynflam. 'you wee-toos are all socialists. this is a plot to take over the colony.'

'what is in it for us,' interjected rogita stones. 'we are getting rich here. we are at the center of colony power.'

general flynflam interrupted. 'you sisters need to take your socialist gasters out of my sight, or we will lock you up.'

at this point, rogita stones started chanting, 'lock them up, lock them up.' as she chanted, her gaster pulsated, causing a giant tattoo of a worm to writhe. the worm was the notorious feniseca tarquinius, the carnivorous caterpillar brought into the colony by corrupt aphid herders. the caterpillar devoured hundreds of nymphs before the plot was discovered and the traitorous aphid herders dismembered. the caterpillar, however, escaped and metamorphized into a butterfly.

rogita stones twisted her gaster around so we could see the tattoo of the disgusting carnivorous worm. 'our god,' she said, and spat a wad of beetle juice at us.

revolted, we retreated to conspire. 'we don't have time to take them to court,' i said.

'agreed, we need direct action now,' said nan. 'we will create a kerfuffle in the nursery and carry off our eggs.'

'okay,' i said. 'i will get a potent colony pheromone from the queen so we can lay down a path to the birdbath. see you there.' we strode off in different directions with determination in our hearts.

nan pelosis recruited councilor kom-millie hairliss. councilor hairliss is the chief civil liberties lawyer for the colony. she enforces laws that keep emergent drones from performing disgusting acts in public, like gaster-scratching and spitting. she also regulates how many drones are produced—just enough to add interest but not too many so as to give listless, lazy, laggard males delusions of dominance. kom-millie hairliss-the-enforcer suffers no fools.

hairliss and pelosis were confronted by a stiff-legged guard at the nursery entrance.

'vot you vant,' commanded the skinny, cadaver-esque ant, whose eyes were turning white.

'since when is there a guard at the nursery. who are you. we are here to rescue the eggs. let us pass,' pelosis and hairliss demanded.

'i am stephanie mill-liar, with a hyphen, taking charge of genetic purity. all eggs locked up and larvae in cages. keeping larvae and eggs safe. not allowing slimy socialist stories to pollute master race of ants. no keys, no entry.'

councilor hairliss was enraged. 'listen, mill-liar, you have no legal authority to cage larvae and eggs. you cannot bar us from the nursery. stand aside, you arrogant pissant. let us pass.'

mill-liar puffed herself up. 'i know you two. you are the troublemakers who take away drone freedoms like scratching in public. you want in, sue me.' then mill-liar began to shout, 'help...socialist attack... arrest them.'

councilor hairliss, refusing to be scared by a stiff-legged, white-eyed, gaster-scratching termagant ant, observed, 'we don't have time for lawsuits. We don't have time for pissants. so here is our direct legal response.' with that she rose up on four legs, reared back her head and thorax, and shot her head forward toward mill-liar's face, catapulting a ghastly gob of millipede goop onto mill-liar's arrogant visage. mill-liar stumbled backward under the force of the masticated legal challenge.

councilor hairliss gave a war-whoop. 'off the pissants.' she and nan pelosis pushed past the flummoxed, gobsmacked stephanie mill-liar. they ran into the nursery shouting, 'attention, nurses, we are under attack. gather eggs and follow us to safety.' nurses rallied to the cause. many recognized kom-millie and nan from the female self-actualization courses they taught. they gathered up eggs and headed toward the exit, only to see it was blocked by mill-liar and a band of white-eyed thugs. our heroines' antennae beat a retreat. 'avast, sisters. to the fire exit. quick. run like tiger beetles. grab our eggs and run.'

nursery ants streamed out of the fire escape following nan pelosis. they bore eggs in their front two legs. in their jaws, they held leaf fragments over their bodies to ward off the rain of spores. this desperate exodus of formicidae refugees carried the next generation of the sweetgum log camponotus carpenter ants. scrambling toward their destiny at the birdbath, they sang, 'follow the pheromone trail.'

meanwhile, i needed to see what help the queen could give us to start a new colony. possibly she could come with us. i

"We don't have time for pissants."

enlisted the help of another wee-too sister, lizbith warwren. she is an ant with a plan, descended from a small colony of the comanche camponotus clan, who migrated east in dried buffalo skins. she became locally famous for inventing a new economy for the former slaves of the strongylognathus slave-makers. Her spirit-name, warwren, means 'little fighter with big songs.' lizbith and i were stopped at the entrance to the royal egg-laying chamber by a big-headed ant with milky eyes and an arrogant frown. she crouched on an enormous gaster. we knew her. this grouchy, immovable fatness was named wilma barrstoole, the self-appointed fixer-to-the-queen. she was feared by most of the department heads in the colony because of her tendency to lock up ants she didn't like.

'let us pass. we need to see the queen. it's an emergency,' we demanded.

barrstoole's response was a gravelly croak. 'no.'

until now, it was normal that anyone could walk in and rub antennae with the queen. after all, it is how her pheromones, and thus leadership, are spread throughout the colony.

when we didn't turn away, barrstoole ground out a rusty so-liloquy. 'nobody sees the queen unless i say. she is the most powerful ant on the planet. i am the most powerful fixer-to-the-queen. we are all-knowing, all-seeing, divine ants on a mission to make this colony the greatest, most magnificent antdom ever. only the queen and her fixer-in-chief can do this. i am the high priestess of magnificence. i know your kind. you are the kind of ants that foment socialist rebellion. you should all be locked up.'

again with the lock-up threat. we were losing patience. we shouted, 'there is an existential threat to the colony. we need pheromones. let us pass. we have ant civil rights.'

her magnificence notched up her croak. 'you have no rights unless i say so. you want pheromones, here, take this.'

we watched barstoole, the magnificent fixer-in-chief, twist her gaster around her fat legs in an attempt to aim her sting in our direction. lizbith boiled over and blurted out an acerbic jibe. 'if you didn't have such a big, bulging, bloated, blimpy, gross, lard-filled, disgusting gaster, maybe that would be easier.'

at this, barrstoole lunged, front legs grasping at lizbith. her antennae knocked lizbith backward. the lunge succeeded in wedging barrstoole sideways in the corridor. she was impossibly stuck. 'quick, let's use the security entrance,' i said. we ran along tunnels to the vertical entrance that accessed the queen's chamber through a trapdoor in the floor.

i eased the trapdoor open. we stuck out our antennae. a moldy, fungal miasma assaulted our senses. the reek of decay hung thick. white cottony threads filled the chamber. the queen lay collapsed, legs splayed, immobile. her eyes were flat white translucent orbs. tiny mushrooms on long stalks sprouted from between her segments. she was wrapped in a cocoon of fungal hyphae. her body was black as a cricket. it seeped sticky, stinking fluids. eggs lay scattered in various stages of putrescence, some leaking fetid fluids. we perceived all this in a brief second, recoiled, and fled through the emergency exit tunnel.

our queen was feeding the fungus, guarded by a fat fixer stuck in a tunnel. the horrible scene from which we had just escaped brought on a wave of nausea. we regurgitated the last day's pill bugs. we were on our own now. this realization and loss of our lunch made us light-headed. our fates were in our own hands, guided by doctor fauchietta's science.

outside, we found a ragged line of nurses. burdened with pearly white eggs, they were winding their way among twigs and grasses toward the birdbath. they were holding leaf fragments over their heads at first, then abandoned them as they emerged from the bane of skylarking infected ants. relieved of their umbrellas, the procession moved faster. we found nan pelosis and kom-millie hairliss in the melee of refugees. kom-millie climbed a grass plant. she waved her antennae to pick up the scent of water. then she pointed three legs in the direction of an enormous white edifice you call a birdbath. nan pelosis marched off in the indicated direction, laying down a pheromone path which the egg-bearers followed. that is how we found the birdbath in your yard.

this goal-oriented march was different than the random walk that your homo sapiens entomologists associate with ant foraging. it is an emergent behavior brought on by the exigencies of survival during a cosmic crisis. watching, i was proud of our leading sisters. if we survive, this behavior will be highly advantageous. i had a revelation. 'i need to figure out how to make them queens so they can pass on their genetic aptitude for intelligent foraging.' but i digress.

when we arrived at the birdbath, lizbith warwren and i related the tragedy of the queen chamber. there would be no pheromones and no rescue for any of the other colony ants. for now, it was imperative we all climb the birdbath and wash off spores we may have carried from the colony. the bath revived our spirits. we are females, so we value cleanliness. most of us are nurses anyway. we splashed. we tossed eggs back and forth. boss, this was probably the first time in 168 million years that ants have actually played. but now it was time to get serious.

we needed to rebuild the colony. nan pelosis, kom-millie hairliss, lizbith warwren, and i assumed leadership of our band of refugees. we numbered about a hundred souls with several hundred eggs. we needed a queen to splash around pheromones that would bind us together and regulate our behavior. we needed to choose a drone. we needed to find a rotten log and rebuild a home. each of us had ideas as to style and decorations. we committed to build back better. before we started, however, we needed rules to keep us safe from the fungus. we found doctor antoinette fauchietta at the edge of the group. she was weak, with milky spots in her eyes. her legs were stiff. we could see she was in the thrall of the deadly fungus. she could barely communicate.

'doctor fauchietta,' i said, 'tell us how to deal with this fungus so it doesn't happen again. but dear doctor, you look sick. what can we do for you.'

the doctor replied, 'i am dying. the psilocybin is taking over. i will give you my final advice.'

'oh no. what are we going to do without you,' we whimpered.

'sisters, there is no cure. watch closely for aberrant behavior.

The first time in 168 million years that ants have actually played

that is the psilocybin taking over. it happens even before lenses in the eyes turn white. any ant under the influence of psilocybin needs to be taken out of the colony and buried before she can skylark and spread sickening spores. no one is immune. this is the inexorable requirement of science-based public health. it is all we can do. remember it well. it applies to everyone. no exceptions.'

we were stunned. our antennae drooped. we stared at the dying doctor fauchietta, who was responsible for saving our colony, as the awful awareness of what we had to do dawned on the four of us.

doctor fauchietta spoke softly. 'you need to...you must... drag me off and bury me...now...before i sprout fruiting bodies...then wash yourselves...remember my advice...i hope you survive.'

with that, doctor fauchietta, our beloved and trusted colony doctor, limped stiff-legged through the grass. the four of us dug a trench. with what little control she still had of her muscles, she lay down and curled up. she tried to draw in her legs, but they twitched. she finally gave up. we buried her. ants are not known for emotions, but we do have them, and mine erupted in a tsunami of grief. sad and shaking, i stood on doctor antoinette fauchietta's burial mound and eulogized.

'here lies the good doctor antoinette fauchietta. in the best tradition of the formicidae class, she gave every molecule of her being to save our eusocial colony. she will be remembered in our genes. she will permeate our thoughts every time we face danger and infection. our progeny owes her its very existence. here lies a true heroine.' i wandered off in a daze.

in the days that followed, the four of us elected kom-millie hairliss to be our new queen. we found an old log and carved out the beginnings of a new home. we built back better. we decorated. the eggs began to hatch. a few were males from which we selected a suitable drone. we sent kom-millie and him on a date. she is now contemplating queenhood. in the past week, we have had to enforce doctor fauchietta's rules only a few times. it was hard. it was heartbreaking. but we did it.

boss, please do us a favor. find our old colony site under the rotting sweetgum log in the woods. you will see thousands of carpenter ants, festooned with mushrooms, hanging from the understory. would you please spray some pesticides around just to make sure no left-behinds survive to spread the disease back to us. you know i don't approve of pesticides, but in this case, it would be merciful and justified. consider it a symbiosis between our two species. we benefit from your horrible technology. you get recycled logs in the woods. and don't forget you have become famous by publishing reports from the only literate carpenter ant on the planet.

in exchange for your extermination service, i will give you some advice based on our recent crisis. i start by quoting a few sentences i found online from a recent book, 'tales from the ant world,' by your celebrated ant guru, professor e.o. wilson. in the second sentence of chapter one he states, 'there is nothing i can even imagine in the lives of ants that we can or should emulate for our own moral betterment.'

later he states, 'ants are easily fooled. they are, after all, only insects, which live by easily exploited instincts.'

as to whose morals to emulate, let me reflect. the infection of corruption and power-lust was more dangerous to us than the fungus because it made us victims of the fungus. but i am living proof that you cannot fool all the ants all the time.

boss, your colony is now experiencing wave after wave of a virus attack. before your species embarks on a moral bender, you should ask how many of your leaders are telling easily fooled humans to do stupid things. Is it possible that homo sapiens has 'easily exploited instincts.'

maybe your virus will teach humans an appreciation of science and nature. maybe ants will get the respect we deserve. is that too much to hope.

with respect for evolution, cindi camponotus, official holly point farm investigative reporter

The Libertarian

july 2021

boss, i met a libertarian this morning who sounded like a socialist and lived like a spider.

nice web, said i.

who is asking, said the orb weaver.

i like the way dewdrops hang on your silk.

you wouldn't if you had to make a living with a net the liberals splashed with water.

whoa, spidey. what is it with the politization of dew. dew is dew. it falls on everyone equally.

Well, look at you, elite little fancy-pants ant. you're one of those socialist colony insects. normally i would be eating you about now. but no. i don't ask anything from anybody. i am libertarian. don't need no government. but what do i get... dew.

what do you think is so unfair, besides dew.

A libertarian who sounded like a socialist and lived like a spider

everyone gets handouts except me. government is planting flowers for butterflies, handing out sugar water to honey-bees, and building houses for migrant birds. meanwhile anyone sees my web, they trash it. that is not fair.

so, as a libertarian you want the government to protect your property.

why not. it's not my fault some snot-nosed urchin busts up my house. somebody's got to pay.

fat chance of that. there are a lot of folks out there who think you are one ugly hombre, with eight hairy legs and eight eyes.

it's not just urchins. birds are the worst. slipshod, sloppy, stupid, stinking socialist birds. i weave warning threads into my web and they blow right through. i heard a warbler bragging to a creeper that he took out my whole orb in one pass.

you want the government to tell warblers where to fly.

absolutely. lock them up if they don't fly right. my civil rights are being violated. the government discriminates against libertarians.

in popularity, you are at the bottom of the polls with assassin bugs.

you are an ant. do you feel the heavy weight of prejudice on your neck squeezing out your vital bodily fluids. i am shocked by squashed spiders.

maybe you need to clean up your act. you run with a crowd

that makes its living by snaring victims in sticky nets, paralyz-ing them, wrapping them like mummies then sucking them dry. and you're shocked by a little prejudice.

there are no rules against the paralyze-package-and-pump caper. this is the purest form of a libertarian free-market lifestyle.

okay, consider your classmates, the widow spiders. The no-tion of being eaten during copulatory consummation sends scary, shocking shivers of dread through all males with ro-mantic tendencies. imagine the juvenile trauma. 'mommy, why are you chewing up daddy. let him go.'

not my problem. it is consensual sexual suicide to get the jump on the competition. now that is freedom.

so, you want the government to take up the cause of libertar-ian spiders. how much tax do you pay anyway.

no taxes from me. i just don't want a bunch of socialist ants, pampered bees, immigrant butterflies and birds getting more handouts than me.

don't you eat migrant butterflies.

suck the juice outta them same as everybody else.

as a libertarian spider then, you're okay with socialist milk-weed subsidies to feed the butterflies you suck dry.

that's right. and while the government is at it, i would like to be treated with respect. quit calling me deplorable.

did you say respect, mister hairy legs. you scare the bejesus out of almost everyone on earth with your fangs, your eight eyes, and your paralyze-and-suck lifestyle. you are defined by the company you keep. worse, you share a class with the ultimate deplorables—chiggers and ticks, who are notorious disseminators of discomfort and disease. they have no fans. none. in fact, many humans who have seen the magnified image of a tick's barbed sucking mouth are driven instantly insane.

okay, the web is drying out. why don't you shimmy up a little closer and let me explain.

boss, it was time to vamoose. seems like everyone wants something from the government, no matter what they call themselves.

with respect for political candor, cindi camponotus, official holly point farm investigative reporter

The Dammed

august 2021

i couldn't see the roiling clouds. but i felt a black squall approaching. it darkened suddenly. cold air blew across the ground. i took shelter under a black oak leaf. raindrops the size of acorns crashed and exploded into showers of droplets as they hit. i ran from under one leaf to another. in the open, i would be drowned. then a blinding flash—bang.

the ground heaved. my exoskeleton rattled. my dna churned. i scented ozone. i scrambled. in front of me, tumbling water thundered and hissed. frothy white. it pounded and beat against rocks in an angry, foaming frenzy. it spilled from a vast hole in the earth. the hole roared and echoed like a giant wounded animal. i climbed on top of the outfall pipe. i hung my antennae over. i was mesmerized by sonorous sounds of cacophony, confusion, and chaos from the deep, dark unknown.

a moan floated above the cataract. it fought its way out of the darkness. i listened. again, it moaned and reformed into the rising notes of a plaintive wail.

'hellllllllllp.'

was this the sound of earth's soul announcing the beginning of the end of homo sapiens. i hoped. it came again. i trembled. i leaned over further. hanging by four legs. antennae pointing into the rushing, cold, wet air. no. this was a terrestrial creature. in trouble. screaming into the other end of the pipe.

i zigzagged over the dam. i ran in the open as the deluge abated. i sensed the vibration of falling water. not the confusion of crashing waves here. only the steady, menacing, sucking roar of a giant vortex.

i started to climb an overhanging tupelo sapling. below me was a drainpipe as big around as a middle-aged sweetgum trunk. it captured and sucked in everything coming within its magnetic current. i climbed higher. my eyes were assaulted by a hilarious, ridiculous, ludicrous, and ominous scene multiplied by my ten thousand lenses. here was the nether end of a large snapping turtle, chelydra serpentina, wedged head down in the vertical drain. his hind legs flailed. his sawtoothed tail swished futilely from side to side.

i edged out so i could see over the pipe. his head hung just above the foam. a waterdrop crashed into me and would have sent me into the maelstrom had i not snagged a stem on the way down. rattled, i licked myself off and assumed an interrogatory position on a less precarious leaf.

i was thinking up some snarky, sarcastic comment to open the conversation when a hen wood duck cruised up. she waddled up to the outfall pipe, stretched her neck over it, and shouted, 'murderer, serves you right.'

'help, get me out of here,' pleaded the turtle.

Mister serpentina, the generally recognized pond bully

'no way. you bit the legs off three of my ducklings, watched them drown, shredded them, and gobbled them. you bloody murderer.'

trying to be authoritative, in spite of his embarrassing position, the turtle replied, 'i obey the laws of nature. the strong multiply and the weak get eaten. i eat anything i want, anytime i want, and nobody sez different. it is survival.'

'well,' retorted the mother duck, 'yer don't fit into that there pipe too well, now do yer. Qua qua qua qua qua,' she chortle-quacked as she paddled away.

i could see her point. i said to mr. serpentina, 'maybe you

could have done with only one duckling. you are a reptile. no reason to overeat. could you at least say you were sorry for being a glutton.'

'never,' said the turtle. 'i am the biggest creature in the pond. i never say sorry. i own this pond. get me outta here.'

What to say to a creature so out of touch with reality that he does not realize he has absolutely no bargaining power. a school of bluegills swam over and circled, some jumping and some standing on their heads in the shallows, splashing with their tails. i said to the turtle, 'the bluegills are mocking you.' all the while the desperate turtle scratched the inside of the pipe with his long, reptilian claws in a vain attempt to make it through to the other side.

i said, 'did it ever occur to you to just back out of that pipe.'

'no,' he replied. 'snapping turtles don't make mistakes. no backing up.' then he growled, 'stinking fish. i will hide in the mud, ambush them, and teach them who is boss of this pond. i'll snap them in two when i get out.'

I had to ask, 'why don't you ask politely. that may soften the hearts and minds of the relatives of the families you have eaten.'

'who are you,' asked the nose-down turtle. 'i can tell from your squeaky little voice you're a nobody. get me out of here or i'll whup your ass.'

splat. a bullfrog, aka rana catesbeiana, jumped out of the weeds and landed in the mud in front of the outfall pipe.

it was missing its left foot. 'crooooooonnnk, looks like you won't be biting any more frog feet. your tadpole-eating days are over. we knew you would destroy yourself. it's your own fault, you stupid bully. croooooooooooooooonk.'

'what do you mean his own fault,' i asked.

the frog explained, 'i saw how it went down. the turtle was creeping up on a leopard frog, mr. rana pipiens, who was sitting on the log in front of the pipe watching damsels. mr. pipiens saw the snapper in time to jump to the edge of the outfall pipe. his gang made sport of jumping into the pipe, riding through to the marsh. he figured he would have some fun with the pond bully, so taunted him, 'catch me if you caaaaaan. hey fat-ass, you can't follow me.' the turtle lunged.'

'the frog plunged. mr. serpentina got stuck, just as the frog expected. a few of us surrounded the turtle and croaked, 'crooooonk—stupid snapper fatso, crooooooooonk—stupid snapper fatso, crooooooooonk—stupid snapper fatso.''

'whoa,' i said, 'is that a nice thing to say to a turtle in mortal danger.'

the response came from another quarter. 'it is not nice. it is highly insensitive. it's fat-shaming. it's disrespectful. it's a violent attack on a turtle's self-esteem. it's sexist and it's horribly anti-reptile.' thus spoke a comparatively svelte, red-bellied cooter, who marched up the bank to the pipe. he stretched his neck and peered over the edge into the water-vortex cascading into the pipe—a foaming funnel just below the snapper's head. the cooter yelled down, 'yo, snapper dude, we have your carapace, big guy. you are not alone. we feel you.'

"Hey fat-ass, you can't follow me."

'well,' i said, 'at last someone takes the side of this dammed snapping turtle. who are you.'

'i am a turtle advocate from 'all turtles matter'. we represent run-over box turtles, trapped terrapins, scandalized stinkpots, reviled red-bellies, the septic soft-shellers, and, of course, our soup-pot snappers. we are members of the testudines order of self-sheltering libertarian reptiles. we are the marginalized minority. we are the never-mascots. we are offended that there are no turtle coins. we are called slow and dimwitted in nursery rhymes. people steer their cars to hit us. we are the victims of millions of years of hunting, entrapment, lies, discrimination, and culinary abuse.'

unable to restrain myself i asked, 'concerning the present company, would that be due to his ugly face and his mud-living lifestyle.'

'we get no respect,' yelled the cooter.

'well, mister cooter,' i retorted, 'there are many of us who are stepped on and abused. Maybe you are just promoting a stewpot grievance culture. what do you do when one of your clan gets stuck in a drainpipe.'

in a condescending tone, the cooter explained, 'we show respect for our brother and sister turtles. we demonstrate. we redistribute blame from the victim to the ecosystem that caused the tragedy, usually built by homo sapiens. then we build a turtle pile at the site and when some big animal comes by, we scram to draw attention to the plight of the, er, dammed, in this case.'

"Yo, snapper dude, we feel you."

'is there anyone who can pull me out,' pleaded the now breathless snapper.

'you are asking the wrong kind of animal,' i said. 'you outweigh me by a factor of two million to one.'

ants are not sentimental, yet i began to feel strangely empathetic. i was the only creature around who could save this dammed beast if i alerted the boss to the plight of this unrepentant, grievance-riddled reptile. chances are that he, being a pity-filled homo sapiens, weighing the appropriate tonnage and having opposable thumbs, would haul the beast out. but ants are not sympathetic creatures. i didn't want the boss to think i was going all sentimentally humane. that would ruin my objective credibility.

i answered the plaintiff, 'mr. serpentina, your attitude sucks. you are a generally recognized pond bully. you are a victim of your own evolution as a solitary cold-blooded species that doesn't give a damn for any of your brothers or sisters. your kind abandon your eggs as soon as you squirt them out. i can't imagine how many lies you have told to lure your victims into snapping range. you don't seem to be acquainted with the golden rule of eusocial communities. you are mean. in truth, mister serpentina, i believe you are a lower form of life than a pill bug. i could save you... but should i.'

'you miserable, anti-testudines, prejudiced, entitled, black-eyed-insect-supremacist monster,' yelled the cooter, his face turning as red as his belly. 'please,' begged the turtle.

'what to do,' i asked myself. 'is it nobler of me to let this turtle suffer the slings and arrows of his outrageous gluttony, ill manners, and disregard for all other creatures, and thus earn his deserved fortune, or to take up arms against this man-made sea of troubles, and by opposing the inevitable, end this turtle's torment.'

'hurry up, you little pest' were mr. serpentina's last mumbled words.

boss, you may ask why you're just hearing about this calamity. call it the fickle finger of fate, the indifference of natural selection, the inexorable arm of justice, or the scourge of revenge. you choose. i could have prevented this. i didn't. rigorously objective eusocial animal that i am, i walked away.

you should remove the corpse from the pond standpipe before it rots and pollutes the marsh.

submitted with respect for the diversity of animals and lived experiences, cindi camponotus, official holly point farm investigative reporter

***Mister serpentina
after the outfall***

The Immigrant

Editor's Note: "The Immigrant" was first published in *The Tatler*, vol. 37, Number 9, October 2022.

february 2022

it was a cold winter day when you dumped me and several hundred of my sisters on an oak log in the ravine in back of your house. dead leaves covered the ground. the forest floor underneath was muddy. green fungi and algae slimed the log. we felt alone in this silent wood.

we were grateful for being rescued from the lethal ophio-cordyceps fungal disease that turned us into zombies back at the farm. here we believed we would be at peace with our surroundings. we expected this to be the promised land. this illusion of tranquility soon disappeared like fog on a warming day, however. a new struggle lay ahead. boss, williamsburg is not the paradise we imagined. it has been a struggle for us, like it has been for any immigrant who stumbles into a new neighborhood, naked, with their eggs and larval progeny. this is an account of our first day, wherein we dealt with poison and murder.

we easily hollowed out a chamber for our queen, kom-millie

We moved from the farm to a new log in Williamsburg

hairliss. we cleared out rotten parts of the oak tree which crossed the stream. she is busy laying hundreds of eggs a day. she spreads the royal pheromone around at concentrations that have inspired us all to build back better. she is turning into a creditable leader of females. she is, however, starting to show a little vanity. carpenter ant queens are usually addressed by their nicknames. but our queen insists on being addressed as 'your excellent queenness.' back in her nursery days, her nickname was 'kommie kid.'

we soon noticed a strange odor in the hollowed chambers. we are sensitive to smells as you know, being able to detect chemicals a million times more diffuse than what is needed to register in your conspicuous homo sapiens beaks. the aroma had a base of benzoquinones with overtones of hydrogen cyanide. it was oaky and putrescent. we heard shuffling feet advancing toward us through the sawdust. a monstrous head pushed through. it was a black dome sprouting two segmented antennae and pinpoint eyes. cleaver-like mandibles chomped at its base. it swayed back and forth, antennae twitching, sensing the air. ten ants long, the beast looked like a segmented sewage pipe and smelled the same. it had hundreds of tiny legs which undulated in waves along its body, plowing it through the sawdust. it squeezed out bundles of frass from its last segment. its mouthparts worked continuously, shoveling in springtails, dead animal parts, fungus, and wood powder. tiny drops of noxious liquid leaked from between its segments as the monster swung from side to side. we had come face-to-face with a diplopoda millipede in the order julida.

this wouldn't do. we had to rid our log of this foul beast. if i couldn't convince it to vamoose, we would have to attack it en masse. that would be ugly. many would be slimed and poisoned. war loomed.

i opened negotiations. 'yo, julida. you are trespassing on royal turf. you need to decamp immediately before the williamsburg community security escorts you out. that won't be pretty.' i didn't know this for sure, but i could envision the scene if a ten-ant-long millipede showed up at the guard office at the campus entrance.

in response, the tuberous terror let out a monstrous burp. 'errrrrrrrrrrrrrrrrrrrrrrrooooooooooooommmmmpft.' apparently, it had no civilized language.

i took charge. 'form up, sisters. we need to roll this monster into the stream.' with superior numbers, we could do this. but the monster would be back. it was going to be an ongoing struggle. then the williamsburg community welcoming committee plopped down, and the situation got dangerous. it landed with a thud in front of our battle line. we retreated to bark crevices.

'welcome to the williamsburg community, little colonials. now line up in triple file so i can take your measure. i need to decide how many of you i can eat in one sitting.'

thus we made the acquaintance of the local ovenbird, seiurus aurocapilla, known for its ravenous appetite for ground-dwelling insects. he sported orange-and-black striped headgear, spectacles, and conspicuous polka dots on his chest. in spite of his nickname, he does not roast his dinner but builds his nest in his oven. i addressed the pugnacious welcomer. 'avast, orange one, you should know that chowing down on a colony of ants full of formic acid will give you serious heartburn.'

'i have no problem with acido balsamico, my little hors d'oeuvres. i have just returned from club med, the land of spicy bugs. my taste buds are burned out. welcome to my hunting ground, my tart tasties. line up. i have an appetite the size of a perdue chicken. wi-chee, wi-chee, wi-chee,' he whooped, with emphasis on the chee.

being seriously outweighed, i tried diplomacy. 'your orangeness, beware who you eat. we have diplomatic immunity in this log. we have paid our dues and are residents of this incorporated socialized community. let's have a truce, and we will show you an arthropod sausage so large you will have difficulty swallowing it.'

he raised his orange crown, brandished his pointed beak above our heads, and let out his preprandial song. 'wi-chee, wi-chee, wi-chee.'

the hairs on my exoskeleton tingled. i had to risk all, or all would be eaten. it was time to unleash the fearless female formicidae genome. i sucked air into my spiracles. i leapt up and yelled the war cry of sister war-wren—descendant of cheyenne camponotus ants who migrated east in buffalo hides—'geeeeerrraaaaaaaaaaaaaaaaaannnnnaaaaaaamooooooo ooooooooooooo.'

i shot under the bird's beak and between his taloned feet. i jumped into the pit of sawdust and grabbed onto a sliver just above julida's head. the bird spun about, belted out a 'wi-cheeeeeeeee,' and jabbed with his scimitar beak. he missed me, but his lower mandible impaled julida in the third segment behind her head. the bird's upper mandible closed tight on the millipede. the ovenbird jerked julida out of the rotten hole. i toppled into sawdust.

the impaled millipede curled, uncurled, and squirmed, flailing back and forth. the bird smashed its foe against ragged bark. thwap, thwap, thwap, thwap. the millipede still wriggled, desperately curling and uncurling. white droplets of noxious fluids and poisonous hydrogen cyanide splattered everywhere. i scampered back to my troops. the ovenbird released his grip for a second. 'wi-cheeeee.' he re-stabbed julida in its nether segments. frass spurted out of julida as the enraged

ovenbird recommenced thrashing its quarry against the oak log—thwap, thwap, thwap, thwap, thwap. blood oozed. the bird released his grip. the millipede lay limp at his feet. orangeness rested, cocking his head and eyeballing his prey with his spectacled red eye. his wings drooped, exhausted.

it was time to capitalize on my act. it was time for negotiation. 'congratulations, orange one. you are an ornithological wonder. your bravery should be rewarded.'

'why are you still here.'

'we hope you enjoy the aromatic sausage we found for you and wonder if you would like more of the same, once you have swallowed this one.'

'quiet, i am eating.'

i ignored this, figuring that orange one couldn't harass us as long as a dripping diplopoda was halfway down his gullet. 'we are good at finding fine fare for feathered friends.'

'don't need your kind of help,' he slurred, beak dripping.

'time comes to feed your brood, you will thank us to point out a gorgeous grasshopper hiding under a leaf or a colony of tasty termites. or would you rather hop around endlessly and aimlessly in the leaf litter while your mate waits at the nest, hungry, hot, and bitchy.'

'how you gonna do that.'

'easy. we have hundreds of scouts. it is what we do. when

we find a critter too big for us, we give you the sign, and you swoop in and make the kill.'

'so i am s'posed to hang on a branch waiting for an ant to wave its little leg.'

'nope. there are lots of you up there. spread the word. one of you will see. could be you. could be your mate. could be a towhee, could be a sparrow.'

'whoa...you bunch of skinny ants plan to feed the whole forest.'

'only the lucky ones. the ones that are watching and are smart enough to know the ant salute. everybody wins. we spot your snacks, and you remove pests from the premises.'

the ovenbird agreed and spread the word.

boss, that is how the 'bird ant treaty organization' was created, otherwise known as 'bato.' it is a beautiful interspecific symbiosis between songbirds and carpenter ants. it isn't perfect, not like diplomatic immunity, but it results in fewer of us being eaten. more foragers make it back to the nest.

an alliance among different species can be useful. you should try it.

submitted with respect for the diversity of animals and lived experiences, cindi camponotus, official williamsburg landing investigative reporter

The Gluttonous Fly

Editor's Note: "The Gluttonous Fly" was first published in *The Tatler*, vol. 38, Number 1, January 2023.

june 2022

operating under the protection of bato—the bird ant treaty organization—has allowed me to extend my territory well beyond the ravine in back of your house, boss. i have begun to explore the 'built environment.' yesterday i ventured out of the woods and on to the sidewalk. that is where i discovered the gluttonous fly.

on the stone-studded sidewalk lay a housefly, musca domestica, on its back with six legs clutching its abdomen, writhing in pain.

'ooooooooooooooooooooooooo. woe is me.'

'my dear diptera, may i assume that your gluttony agrees not with your innards. what vile vittles have brought you so low. have you licked up a supersized helping of pathogenic microbes.'

'noooooooooooooooooo. it's the syrup. i drank the whole

"I assume that your gluttony agrees not with your innards?"

puddle. the desserts are sooooo good in there. i can't help myself.'

i thought i would never see a fly get sick from what it ate. but here was proof—lying on its back, dying of gluttony. but his doom was my boon. knowing that he was filled with glucose instead of germs, i climbed up on a stone to scout the best path to drag his whimpering carcass across the concrete to our log. by then he would be freshly dead, al dente and delectable. mister housefly would be distributed to the colony by our fly knackers. i was deciding how to get a grip on the dolorous dipterous dude when...

boom. the earth shook. then a scream,

'jump...now.'

i looked up. yikes. an enormous leather shoe floating above the pavement was headed for me at decapitation level. i jumped in the direction of the shout and grabbed onto gaberdine overhanging another leather shoe. it levitated, arced up, forward and down again. 'hold on, mate, we are in for rough seas. heave yerself over the transom. hang on. enjoy the ride. we are headed to the land of plenty.'

poking over the edge of a navy-blue cuff, i looked back and beheld a smear of chitin on concrete—what was left of the gluttonous housefly and what would be me if it were not for the black-and-yellow big-eyed flower fly, milesia virginiensis, now peering at me from her fabric stronghold. i looked out at the world that lurched in arcs with the rhythmic motion of nauseating sea swells. 'thanks for the warning, milesia. but for your hail, my literary career would be over. now i am going to be seasick.' i upchucked down the deep blue fabric.

'well, mate, we all need a little help. i figure we are neighbors now. we need to help each other. especially them that is disabled.'

'yes, i see you have a missing wing.'

'the result of an encounter with an ovenbird with a bad aim. lopped off one o' me wings.'

'i know that bird. we narrowly escaped, ourselves. so what is a yellowjacket mimic doing riding in an old man's cuff.'

'well, i cannot hover above blooms anymore, so i have to dine at the kitchen yonder. it is too long a voyage to leg it, so i hitch a ride to the land o' plenty and back again to my garden blooms, where i spend the night.'

'why don't you just stay there.'

'i can see you need to learn about kitchen etiquette. you get caught napping in a pool of syrup—first you get the flyswatter and then they spread poison underneath everything. remember, if you cannot see their eyes, they cannot see you. best to eat your fill and skedaddle before the terrorist lady with the broom starts whacking away under the stove.'

'how do you get back.'

'easy. the slow shoes are always a round trip. just eat your way around under the counters and hop back in for the ride home. jump off when the ship passes your pheromone trail.'

thus began our adventure in your kitchen, boss. we have formed a daily kitchen forage patrol. you octogenarians are a friendly lot so don't mind a few stowaways. we limit our numbers, however, so as not to invoke a poisonous immune response among your xenophobic kitchen staff. if you hear any blowback about 'ant infestation,' tell them we are cleaning up crumbs and not leaving flyspecks.

our patrols try to maintain a high-protein diet. several sisters who could not control their sweet cravings, however, ended up sugar-shocked with bloated gasters. some died of formicidae glucosidis. let that be a lesson to you, boss. you may be able to ingest a whole cake, but it will eventually kill you. in the event you do eat the whole thing, i suggest you regurgitate to your nestmates when you return from the kitchen.

thanks to you, we are in a wood free of zombies. we are immigrants trying to fit into a new ecosystem. this may turn out to be the promised land after all, but it will take an effort. we will do whatever it takes to prosper. we will clear your woods of carcasses, help sequester carbon in your soils, and control household arthropods that make your females scream. i will report on events in your neighborhood. but a quid pro quo is required. for now, this includes a ban on the use of insecticides in your woods and especially in the kitchen. in return we will not eat your homes.

keep our headquarters secret. if anyone mentions 'ants,' tell them that their neighborhood is now an historical site. it is home to a colony of carpenter ants whose ancestors have taught them how to survive for a hundred and sixty-eight million years through volcanic hell, high water, and continental drift. also, they should be happy to have their own investigative reporter who can crawl under the litter and report the truth.

submitted with respect for the diversity of animals and lived experiences, cindi camponotus, official williamsburg landing investigative reporter

Bear Attack

Editor's Note: This story ("Marauding Bear on Campus") was first published in *The Tatler*, vol. 37, Number 8, September 2022.

The usual modus operandi of the "animal control" department in Williamsburg for wandering bears, lacking a bloody mauling, is to track culprits. They inform Homo sapiens to take in their bird feeders, lock up trash cans, and wait out the marauder until the bear has passed out of the neighborhood and back into the woods. Any suggestions to the authorities that the bear may be suffering from family separation, spatial disorientation, or could be disabled have fallen on deaf ears. There is therefore almost no chance that our bear visitor will be allowed into assisted living or even given a session in the physical rehabilitation facility in our continuing care community.

In her following report, Cindi is attempting to respect the bear's gender identity, having never asked its sex. I find this annoying and a waste of ink and electrons. In the future, I will edit out this nonsense.

august 12, 2022

we were attacked by a bear. i thought this was a more civilized community than your farm in the middle-of-nowhere, boss. i was wrong.

this morning, a large, lumbering black bear shambling through the woods smelled our nursery. he/she/it proceeded to tear it apart with his/her/its unmanicured claws. lucky for us, we built back better when you dropped us here last winter. we sequestered the nursery in the heartwood. he/she/it couldn't beach our security, so shuffled off up the hill toward your house.

i jumped into the fur of his/her/its back. this was going to be exciting. i felt like a reporter in a war zone. it smelled like it too. this bear hadn't bathed in months. and his/her/its pelt was crawling with fleas and ticks.

as i was reconsidering the life of a correspondent in a war zone, the ride got bumpy. the bear attacked your bird feeder. he/she/it rose up, grabbed the pole, and thrashed it side to side. he/she/it bent the pole over, grabbed the big feeder, and attempted to pull himself/herself/itself up to it. the bear continued to worry the pole, grunting and swearing bear oaths. the pole finally broke. feeder and bear crashed to the ground. i fell from his/her/its unwashed fur. he/she/it punctured one feeder with his/her/its ivory ursine canines and tore the other one apart on the ground with his/her/its claws.

he/she/it clearly had no respect for private property.

after licking up the seeds, he/she/it finally lumbered off. he/she/it was injured. one back leg was stiff and the other caused a skip. his/her/its gait resembled one of your peg-legged pirates. it was worse than yours, boss. like you, he/she/it could use some physical therapy. or maybe he/she/it was already in rehabilitation and got thrown out for eating folks' lunches.

you should suggest to management that this bear be moved to assisted living where he/she/it will be fed regularly until he/she/it recovers. there is no reason why a resident in our continuing care community should have to shamble about at night tearing apart logs and vandalizing bird feeders. show some of your golden rule empathy. it will be sunday tomorrow and your good samaritan act will make you feel righteous in church.

submitted with respect for the diversity of animals and lived experiences, cindi camponotus, official williamsburg landing investigative reporter

Ingram Content Group UK Ltd.
Milton Keynes UK
UKHW040717170423
420292UK00004B/228